# ROSE KNOT

NP Novellas:

# ROSE KNOT

## A Tale of the Rose Knight

### Kari Sperring

NewCon Press
England

First published in the UK August 2021 by
NewCon Press
41 Wheatsheaf Road,
Alconbury Weston,
Cambs, PE28 4LF

NPN009 (limited edition hardback)
NPN010 (paperback)

10 9 8 7 6 5 4 3 2 1

ISBN:

978-1-912950-92-8 (hardback)
978-1-912950-93-5 (paperback)

Cover layout and design by Ian Whates
Incorporating an image by Duncan Kay

Typesetting and editorial meddling by Ian Whates
Text layout by Ian Whates

# Prelude

I suppose that it started with Essyllt. Or then again, perhaps not. Perhaps, like so much else, it started with Lamorak de Galis. It would be easy to blame Lamorak. He's dead and gone, with no one at hand to speak up for him. But they say it's unlucky to speak ill of the dead. And from what little I know of Lamorak, he's unlikely to have thought beyond the immediate effect of his action. Perhaps I should learn to wish that he had never met that monk. Perhaps then I could tell myself that none of this would ever have come to pass.

It takes a particular kind of mind to lie to oneself. My sister Luned would have no difficulty at all. But I just don't have the heart. It would have happened, most of it, come what may. There's a shadow which follows my husband's kin: Lamorak was no more than another eclipse, brought down in the darkness we do not name.

I am Llinos of Kinkenadron, wife to Sir Gareth of Orkney, and this is my testament. Read it as you will. It is my truth. I seek no forgiveness, I offer no revelation. It began for me on a cool autumn evening at Camelot. It began with my cousin-by-marriage, the Queen of Cornwall, lovely Essyllt.

# One

"Well," Essyllt said, "I wouldn't put up with it." She pressed the last pin into the net which held up her hair, and picked up her silver-bound mirror. "I'd do something about it right away: be sure of that." She paused a moment, gazing at her reflection. Then her brows drew together. "Do you think I'll do?"

In the warm light of the candles, her beauty was quite startling. The heavy mass of apricot hair was woven with pearls no whiter than her skin and her spring-green gown held her like a lover. The very sight of her made me smile. "Of course you will."

"Really?" She hesitated. "I'm trusting you, Llinos, so you have to tell me truthfully." She put down the mirror, and turned. "You must be completely honest. I can handle it. At least, I think I can… There are so many beauties here, what with the queen of Logres, and Lady Enide, and Laudine, and you, of course, so I… Well, go ahead, tell me." She straightened her shoulders, the defendant before the judge, and looked straight in the eyes. "Go on."

I had to control an impulse to laugh. "You're beautiful. As usual."

"Oh, praise heaven!" Essyllt rolled her eyes in deliciously comic relief. "I'm always on such pins whenever I come here, between one thing and another. Marcus frets me, and makes me forget half my baggage, and then Guenever… I know she doesn't mean it, but somehow she always manages to make me feel as if I dye my hair." Crossing the small room, she sat down beside me, and kissed my cheek. "I do miss having you amongst my ladies, love. I wish that husband of yours would let you come back to Cornwall."

"Gareth likes to be near his uncle."

"Yes, I know." She leant over, and took my embroidery out of my hands. "You're so pretty, and you know how to make everyone so comfortable, so of course he wants to keep you with him. But I want to be selfish and keep you too."

"Not so pretty after the baby." I looked from her trim waist to my own. "I'm growing sadly dumpy."

"No, you're not, love. You just let people neglect you." She looked wicked. "I've a good mind to steal you, and take you home with me to be pampered. That Gareth of yours is neglecting you shamefully. And so I shall tell him, if I get half the chance."

"He's busy, that's all."

"Well, he has no right to be." Abruptly she leapt to her feet. "I'm going to make you beautiful for him. Or for someone else, if he's too busy to look."

"Essyllt!"

"No, you're not shocked. I can tell when you're pretending. I'm in the mood for sorting people out. Now, tell me: *is* there someone who's caught your eye?"

"I love Gareth."

"I know, lovey – and so does half Logres, after those silly chastity tests – but it won't hurt to stir him up a bit." She lowered her lashes, and looked coy. "A little jealousy can work wonders in affairs of the heart."

"I don't know…"

"Well, I do." She pulled me to my feet, and looked me up and down.

"Do let me, Llinos. It'll be fun, I promise." Her voice was pleading. I tried to shake my head at her, but found myself laughing instead. She smiled. "I knew you would." Drawing me over to her dressing chest, she picked up a brush, and began to take down my hair. "Look at all this. Mine will never behave, or stay tidy. We'll show it off, and we'll take you out of at least one of those petticoats. You don't need them with the fires in the hall, anyway. Then we'll see who is and isn't looking."

Her hands moved quickly skilfully, braiding my front hair, leaving the remainder to fall loose down my back, like a maiden's. "What colour were you wearing when you first met your Gareth? I know you remember, so don't try to tell me you don't."

"I won't, then. It was white. But…"

"White it shall be. I have just the gown. Context is very important. I only have to wear a little rosewater around Tris, and…" She broke off, laughing. "It works like magic."

"Essyllt, you're so careless." It was easy to be fond of her; easy to love her, too. But she worried me. She had no discretion. "After that incident with the monk and the chastity test."

She sighed. "I know, lovey. I do try, but somehow I can never remember to be really cautious." Her face brightened. "And I avoided the test well enough, didn't I, and no harm done. If Lamorak de Galis had any real sense of honour, he would never have let that monk take that horrid thing anywhere. But I suppose one can't expect anything better from a man of his kind." She was frowning. That made me nervous.

I said "Lamorak's very young. And…" I hesitated. Then: "I'm sure he meant no dishonour to you. I think he was just trying to get back at Tristan."

It was quite the wrong thing to say. Her lovely eyes narrowed. She said "And just what is Tris supposed to have done to him?"

Insulted my brother-in-law. But that was not a matter to raise with indiscreet Essyllt. I shrugged, and said "'I've no idea. Some joust or other, I expect."

"Tris *is* very skilled at jousting." Essyllt seemed ready enough to let the matter lie. She smiled at me, and added, "You mustn't worry. I'll be all right. Truly, Marcus doesn't care over-much what I do, so long as he can spend time with Andred. I don't know what I'd do if he behaved like some of the courtiers here: your Agravaine, for instance. I believe he takes those tests *seriously*. His poor wife!" Her blue eyes danced. "Perhaps I should light a candle in gratitude for a complacent husband."

"Oh, Essyllt!" Despite myself, I was laughing. "It really isn't funny."

"I know it! All those hypocrite men testing us with magical robes and cups, and looking supercilious. And hardly a one of them with even a shadow of a claim to the moral high ground." She twisted a silver pin into my hair, and looked pensive. "And a good thing, too."

She sounded as if she might be plotting something. I said carefully, "Why?"

Her expression became demure. "Well, Tris is in France – and playing up to half the women at Claudas' court, if I know him – and Marcus isn't interested. I have to amuse myself somehow while I'm here."

"You're incorrigible."

"I'm made like that, I can't help it." Again, that wicked light in her eyes. "Maybe I should lead that horrid Lamorak on. Serve him right if I broke his heart."

I thought about Lamorak de Galis, with his yellow snake's eyes, and smooth manners. A good man in the lists, my husband said, but wild. Other rumours around the court linked him with my mother-in-law, the treacherous queen of Orkney. Essyllt would be no match for Margawse. I said "I don't think that would be a good idea."

"Oh?" Essyllt looked intrigued. And then "Don't tell me the stories are true? I thought that was just more of Andred' s nonsense." My concern must have shown, for she added, "Lamorak's supposed to have some dark unrequited. passion. Something utterly mysterious and perverted."

All of those were words I could find quite apt for my mother-in-law. But then there was that happy word unrequited. It was probable that even Agravaine would overlook an unfulfilled love for his mother. I looked down, hastily, and said "I don't know about that. I just meant that Lamorak is flighty. I don't believe he cares for much at all, apart from knighthood." Sometimes, it can be a burden, being a step-Orkney. So many sore places to avoid.

"Oh, another one." Essyllt was dismissive. "Well, it runs in his family, I suppose. His brother Percevale is an absolute prig." She put her hands on my shoulders. "Still, there's no shortage of more interesting men here, anyway." She kissed my cheek.

That made me laugh again. "Oh, Essyllt!"

"No, you can't possibly understand. You're loyal, and sensible, and good, and married to lovely Gareth, who adores you (when he remembers). Whereas I'm just incurably frivolous." Her tone was unexpectedly serious.

I half-turned, and caught her hand. "You're not unhappy?"

"What?" She shook her head. "No, lovey, I'm just restless. I need to find someone to play with: I'm tired of being grown up and responsible, and Tris is getting so possessive. I'm counting on you to help me find a playmate."

"Me?"

"Who else? You know everyone here, and they all love you. You can put me on to the good ones." She took her hand away, and went to her clothes' press. Opening it, she began to rummage. "That dress should be in here: I know I packed it. So, tell me about that delicious brother-in-law of yours."

"Which one? I have four, in case you hadn't noticed."

"Who could miss them? The Orkneys, such glorious specimens of manhood! It makes me quite dizzy to think about it." She re-emerged from the closet, clutching a cream over-gown, and a pair of matching sleeves. "I'm sure this will fit. Let me help you." She spun me round, and started on the lacing of my bodice. "Anyway, what do you make of my chances with your delectable kinsman?"

"You still haven't told me which one. If it's Gawain..."

She paused, holding one of my skirt tags in her hand. "Ah, Gawain. Beautiful, attainable, and fickle as a breeze. He's a dream, of course, but who can hold him? No, I meant the big one."

"The big one?" For a moment, I couldn't think who she meant. Then "Gaheris?" I looked back at her over my shoulder. "Not Gaheris?"

"Don't look so surprised. Why not?"

"Well, I..."

"It's not as if your sister has any real use for him. (Do you know who it is she's involved with at present? I'd love to know.) And I only want to borrow him." She looked wicked. "You know, I think he's almost bigger than Tristan." Her tone was light, but her expression lent ready scandal to her meaning. "What do you think?" I looked unconvinced. She continued "Does he have some terrible secret?"

"Not that I know of." I hesitated, then turned properly, and faced her. "I wish you wouldn't."

She sighed. "Don't disapprove of me, Llinos, please."

"I don't. It's just... Well, Heris is shy, and..."

"Still waters run deep."

"I daresay, but the fact is he doesn't get on with your Tristan, and I'd hate for the two of them to fight. Heris would lose, and then the rest of the clan would get all riled up on his behalf, and... "

"Yes, I see." Essyllt was briefly serious. "The Orkneys never forget." She shrugged. "Well, it was just an idea. Luned threw such a wobbly about him after the mantle test last month that I thought there must be something..."

My sister Luned has never been good at hiding her feelings. I waited for Essyllt to finish pulling the cream gown up over my shoulders. Then I said, "That was Agravaine's fault, really. He made such a huge scene about Laurel failing the test that Luned felt slighted. Heris is her husband, after all, yet he didn't say a word. She said he didn't even value her enough to be angry, he just looked resigned."

"Oh, poor Luned!" Essyllt caught my eye, and giggled. "'That *is* rather deflating."

"I know, but she'd have been even more upset if he'd beaten her, as Agravaine did Laurel."

"I'm beginning to feel sorry for the delightful Gaheris."

"Essyllt..."

"I know, I know, I'll leave him alone, I promise. But I do think we should try turning the tables on Agravaine and his ilk. In fact, I'm beginning to have rather a good idea about that..." She gave a final tug on my laces, and began to tie them. "'There. I've always said front-lacing gowns are the most flattering. Look at yourself." She picked up the mirror, and held it where I could see. The dress was a little on the tight side. It did interesting things for my bust. Essyllt said "You look lovely. "

I reached over, and kissed her. ""Thank you."

"You're welcome." She smiled. "I shall speak to Brangwen about my idea… Shall we go down and stun the courtiers?" Her arm slipped about my waist. "I'll only be a little naughty, I promise. Now, tell me what you think of Kay."

"Beautifully brusque. But he isn't here: he went with the king to London."

Essyllt pretended to pout. "Everything's against; me! I suppose it will just have to be Gawain, then." She sighed, and placed a hand over her heart. "Oh, the burden of it!"

"You'll survive," I said, smiling.

"I know, love," she said. "And knowing Prince Gawain, I'll enjoy it."

I could be melodramatic, and say that that was the last night on which I remember seeing my husband and his brothers all together in harmony, but I don't know if it would be true. Distance lends everything a gloss. More likely there were the same petty frictions and jealousies which in the end tore us all down. I remember coming to the foot of the stair with Essyllt to find them all grouped together at one end of the hall, neat and uncomfortable in their finery. "Holy Virgin!" said Essyllt into my ear. "The people of the hills. Don't they ever intimidate you? One forgets there are so many."

Malicious tongues credit my mother-in-law with finding a different father for each of her children. Perhaps it was true: I've never known. Certainly, no one could have told it by looking at her sons. They all looked like her, with that rich brown hair that is red under strong sun, long, big bones, and dark eyes. Gawain is the darkest, and many think him the handsomest, too, with his spare frame and sleepy, slow smile. He has a quick temper and a kind heart, and he notices everything. That night, he stood in the centre as always, looking down the hall towards the queen, whom he was officially escorting. Agravaine stood to his left, a little shorter than Gawain, and a little broader, with hair the exact same russet shade as his mother's. He was laughing, showing his fine teeth. My Gareth beside him was laughing too, the fairest and slightest of all the family. His hair needed cutting: he'd been on at me for weeks to trim it, but I'd resisted. It hung to his shoulder blades, a little untidy, two shades lighter than Agravaine's. Medraut was to Gawain's right, composed and still. He's as dark as Gawain, and not done, quite, with growing. He stood almost as tall as Gaheris, who's the tallest man at court, saving only Kay. Gaheris himself stood, as ever, at the back, mainly in shadow, as if he would disguise his size. Alone among the brothers, he has grey eyes, not brown. I'd thought perhaps he had them of Lot of Orkney, but my cousin Marcus, who's old enough to know, told me Gaheris was the image of his maternal grandsire, Duke Gorlois. That Cornish blood runs strong, swamping all other humours which come in its way. I've a little of it myself, and both Luned and I are as dark as Medraut and Gawain. The bishop had frowned, marrying Gareth to me. Cousins in the third degree, too close for comfort and refusing from love to await the Roman dispensation. But I'd have wed Gareth anyway, whatever the church required: over the broom if necessary. I stood there by the stair, watching him, content and complete, and Essyllt laughed, looking at me. Then Gawain noticed us, and prodded Gareth.

No, it was an evening like any other, arranged by the queen for the amusement of herself and her guests. A light supper, and then the covers were drawn, and the musicians came in for the dancing. Medraut kissed my fingers behind a pillar, and whispered "Why didn't you keep a sister or cousin for me, Llinos?", and, a little drunk, I only smiled, and kissed his cheek. I'd lost Essyllt long before, whisked into the circle by someone or other. I was dizzy and breathless, and when the music ended, sought refuge on one of the long benches. Gareth was leading out the queen: across the room, we caught each other's eyes, and smiled. Beyond him, I saw Luned, flirting with two or three of the younger knights.

From my left a voice said, "You look hot, Lady Llinos. May I fetch you something?" I turned. It was Lamorak de Galis. His left arm was in a sling; looking at me, he bowed and added, "I can't dance, as you see, but I can make myself useful fetching and carrying." He smiled. "It's important to be useful, don't you think?"

"Very probably."

"Gaheris says I'm dreadfully underfoot." His smile turned rueful, and he drew up a stool. "May I? Or shall I bring you wine?"

"If I drink any more I'll be paying for it all tomorrow." I rather liked Lamorak, what little I knew of him. I could afford to: I had Gareth. I was immune to others' charms. I smiled at him.

He sat. "How lovely you look," he said, easily. "Sir Gareth is lucky." He had probably said very similar things to more or less every other woman present. I looked at him steadily, and after a moment he looked down. He said, "You know, I can talk nonsense by the hour. But not to you. You're very serious, Lady Llinos."

Sensible, Essyllt had said, but it amounted to the same thing. I watched her for an instant, dancing with Gawain. Her eyes were very bright. He was smiling. Accomplished, the pair of them, in the art of dalliance, ready to play and walk away. Lamorak followed my gaze. He said "Now that lady isn't serious at all."

"Only in her displeasure." I turned back to him. "It isn't for me to mention it, but…"

Lamorak held up a hand. "No. I called you serious. I deserve it." He was trying to make me smile. He really was very young, and something about him was vulnerable. Too young by far for Margawse, who can cow even Kay with a look. Lamorak was smiling, but it didn't reach his eyes. He said, "It's that business with the monk, isn't it? It was a terrible thing I did. I wouldn't blame her if she sent her men after my head." He looked down. "I could say I wasn't thinking, but it wouldn't be true. I'd had an argument – a dreadful one – with Tristan, and I felt like killing him. When the monk appeared with his magical test of female constancy, all I saw was a chance to humiliate Tris. I didn't even think about what it might mean for Queen Essyllt... I'm glad she avoided it. I should never have sent the monk in the first place." He paused and drew a breath. "Gaheris says I should apologise."

"Gaheris is right." But something in Lamorak's voice troubled me. His face was averted. I said, "Is something wrong?"

"Good heavens, no!" He laughed without turning. "Just cowardice. I'm terrified of the Queen of Cornwall. Impressive, don't you think, in a fighting man? Do you think she'll poison me?"

"She's more likely to try and break your heart." Lamorak's head snapped up, and he stared at me, startled. I was fairly surprised at myself. "Essyllt doesn't bear grudges, not really. But you insulted her, and she doesn't know why."

"I do everything wrong." He shook his head. "Gaheris says I forget to think." I was silent. He rubbed a hand along his bandaged arm. "I suppose it won't help if I tell her the truth?"

"I don't know."

He looked away again. "She's very beautiful," he said, and sighed. "But she can't break my heart." He was not watching Essyllt. His face was sad. He was staring at the other side of the hall, at my sister Luned, and her coterie, and beyond, at the tall shape of my brother-in-law Gaheris, standing silent in the shadows.

# Two

Sometime after midnight, Gareth lifted his head from my shoulder, and said "I saw you talking to Lamorak de Galis."

I was warm, and content, and more than part asleep. My husband had been very taken with my borrowed dress. I opened my eyes a little, and said "Hmm?"

"He worries me." Gareth said.

"Why?" He was silent. I added "You're not jealous?"

"What?" He looked startled. "No, sweetling. I trust you." He kissed my brow. "It's just Lamorak... He attracts trouble." He hesitated. "Heris says he'll grow out of it... What is it?"

"Lamorak. You reminded me – he kept saying that, too: 'Gaheris says'."

"I don't like it," Gareth said. "I keep thinking something bad will happen."

A little over two months later, my mother-in-law died by violence. No one seemed clear as to the how or the why, although it was Gaheris who stood trial for the deed. The Orkneys quarrelled bitterly, before dividing along familiar lines. Gawain and Gaheris. Agravaine and Medraut. Gareth trapped helplessly between them, unable to mediate, miserable, confused. Lamorak de Galis had vanished from court the night of the murder, and no one knew the reason for that, either. "Perhaps," Luned said, maliciously, before the whole court, "he's trying to protect *your* good name, Heris." Gaheris, quieter than ever, could not meet her eyes. He would not defend himself, not even at the request of the king. He would not talk about it at all, except to repeat over and over, "It was my fault."

It could not be proved either way. The trial ended nothing; Agravaine muttered darkly about Lamorak. And within a half a year, Lamorak too was dead.

I barely registered the fact. A month before, Gareth and I had lost our baby, our only child. There was no tragedy to touch it. I fled the court, home to Kinkenadron, where no one murmured or looked; and Gareth stayed behind. Those days are not, even now, to be spoken of. I could not bear myself, for living when my child did not. The world held no solace: not even Gareth understood. He had duties at court, business, family quarrels. I had nothing. We could not even comfort each other. When Gareth came west to the domain, we found we had nothing to say. Each time he left, I wept, yet I could neither talk to him nor follow him. And the intervals between his visits and letters grew longer.

Not wholly his fault. He at least made attempts to come to me. I made none whatsoever to go to him. I was lonely, there in Kinkenadron, yet I lacked the energy to mend the condition. Queen Guenever sought me to return to court for Christmas, and I pleaded off. In February, Medraut came to the domain alone, and stayed a night or two. He'd grown a beard, and was beginning to fill out to match his height. I barely listened to his fund of witty, clever stories of the court. It was nothing to me, who loved whom, who lived and who died, aside from my one child. "How pale you are," said Medraut, taking my hand. "More fool Gareth, leaving you here alone."

"I like it." And I would have withdrawn my hand, but he was the stronger.

He said, carefully, "There is a terrible pain in this family. Gareth... There has been something said, between Gareth and Gaheris. You should come back to court, Llinos."

But I did not heed him. The Orkneys were forever at odds with each other. I would not recall that Gareth, over all, forbore to quarrel with his brothers. Heris, at least, had the Orkney temper. It would pass, all earthly things passed. I remained alone at Kinkenadron until it was almost spring. Almost a year since the loss of my little girl. Mid-March brought another letter from the queen: no request, now, but a command. I must attend her at Easter, she would brook no excuse. She had sent my half-brother to fetch me: I must be escorted, we must travel the long way round. A shadow lay on Surluse forest in late days; there were strange stories, rumours of fell creatures and worse. Some claimed a ghost knight had been seen riding there. The queen would expose me to no dangers. Dutifully, I packed my chests, and Gringamore and I made the long journey back to Camelot.

I felt rather like a ghost myself. I had nothing to say to my companions, to the queen, to her ladies. At night I lay away from Gareth, my face to the wall.

I had entirely forgotten Essyllt and her half-laughing schemes of vengeance. I lived now in another world. I think I did not even look up fully when the green-clad damsel came before the queen.

She bore a rosewood box: with a deep reverence, she laid it at Guenever's feet. "A gift, madame, from the queen of Cornwall."

Guenever smiled, and took the box. The lid was plain. She opened it, and frowned. Within lay a silver-bound hunting horn.

"It is magical, my lady," the damsel said. "A species of game. The horn may be sounded only by he who has remained faithful to his lady for the past year and a day."

Slowly, the queen said "This tests male fidelity?"

"Yes, my lady."

There was a small silence. Someone giggled. Guenever smiled. Her fingers drummed on the edge of the box. "Well, she said, softly, "trust Essyllt." She looked across at Andrivete, Kay's wife and head of her household. "I think," she said, "that we must hold a special supper party."

It did not occur to me that the plan could in anyway affect me. A game, no more, and one which seemed to touch on nothing of any importance. The queen laid her plans quickly, and swore us all to secrecy. It was almost May: Easter had come late this year. What season could be more appropriate? We would ride out for the Maying, and end the celebration with a small, exclusive supper in the Queen's large chamber. The men should be told nothing: the ladies would lead them blind into the test, as the knights themselves had formerly led their ladies. "And about time, too!" said my soft-voiced cousin Laurel. She wore only high-necked gowns, to hide the scarring on her shoulders. Agravaine was an unforgiving husband. "Let those hypocrites suffer, for once." She looked down. "I expect Agravaine will beat me for not warning him, but it will be worth it to see him fail."

"You're so sure he's unfaithful?" asked Alis, the new bride, a little shocked. "It's worth risking his anger?"

"Who knows?" said Luned. She smiled. "We might all be in for a few surprises."

Mayday was bright and clear. There was laughter as we rode through the cool green woods. Laurel had talked me into colours: the first time for a year. There was no wind. It might almost have been summer, there amidst the trees. Someone started up a song. The voices rose clear, if not always true, verses traded back and forth between men and women. Gareth looked at me as he sang, and I wished suddenly that we were alone. He looked tired: something was troubling him, and I had taken no account of it. How long since we had exchanged more than formalities? Six months? Ten? I turned my horse's head towards him, but the queen suddenly spurred on into the wood and I had to follow. The men pursued us, laughing, as we collected the May blossoms. Later, we gathered on the river bank for refreshment and more music. When I looked around for Gareth, he was nowhere to be seen. I remembered again that my child was dead, and for me the sun went in.

Gaheris settled on the bank beside me, a cup of ale in either hand. There was a dark mark all along one of his cheekbones, like dirt, or a bruise. He saw me looking, and said "I was careless in the practice yard. Kay always says I lumber like a camel." And then, "You're not singing."

"Neither are you," I pointed out.

He grinned. "If my life depended on my carrying a tune, I'd be sending for a coffin-maker."

"I don't feel like singing."

"No. Poor Llinos." He looked at me a moment, then added, "It's good you're back with us. Gareth was miserable without you."

"Then where is he now?" I said, and looked down.

"Someone's horse cast a shoe. You know Gareth: he always has to help those in trouble." Gaheris put the ale down, leant back on his elbows, and crossed his ankles. "He'll be along soon, I daresay. Or you might ask Gavin to go and look for him."

"Not you?"

He avoided my eyes, gazing up at the sky. "I'm too lazy today."

"You know, Heris," I said, slowly, "Medraut came to see me at Kinkenadron." Gaheris was silent. "He told me that you'd quarrelled, you and Gareth."

"Mouse has a loose tongue." He stopped, then sat up. "He didn't need to trouble you with that. It was nothing."

But Gareth was unhappy... Medraut was right, I should have returned sooner. I looked across at Gaheris. "Has something happened?"

"No," he said. Then he flushed, and went on, "Just me making a fool of myself. The usual. It doesn't matter, now you're with us again."

The sun was low when we returned to the castle: there was a terrible flurry to wash and tidy up for the queen's supper. My sister Luned snapped as the maid tried to brush out her hair, then quite suddenly dissolved into tears. I sent the girl away, and tried to comfort her, but she would have none of it. "You don't understand," she said furiously. "You never could."

We went down together in silence. As we gathered in the solar, Andrivete looked at the queen. "You don't have to go through with this."

Guenever bit her lip. Then she shook her head. "And have Essyllt say ever after that I was afraid to play the men at their own game? No. It will be done."

"There will be trouble from it," Andrivete said.

"As there was trouble over Dame Morgan's mantle?" Guenever said. She looked across at Laurel, who lowered her eyes. "Let there be."

The hall was bright with candles, and fragrant with the May. Over the courses, the guests grew merry. Gareth and I shared one dish, and his hands were warm on mine. The light seemed to be everywhere, filling my eyes. The shadow was beginning, perhaps, to go its way. To my left, Gawain paid meticulous, insincere court to the queen, who laughed at him. Across the table, Luned stared into her lap, and kept her face averted from her neighbours. The king was at Winchester with Lancelot and the bishops. It occurred to me that Guenever would not have played this trick had the king been present.

"Llinos," Gawain said suddenly, "I appeal to you. Her majesty calls me a frippery thing: please defend me."

Gareth peered at him over my shoulder. "Not frippery, surely? The amount you eat, Gavin, you're too big to be a trimming."

Gawain bowed to him. "Attacked on both sides," he said, ruefully. "I'm the eldest, Gari. Have you no respect?"

"Over dinner?" said Gareth. "No."

"You see," said the queen, "false coin will out." Gawain put his elbows on the table, and laughed.

Guenever smiled. Then she clapped her hands, and the servants came in to draw the covers. As they went out, she rose and called her ladies to her. We stood at her shoulders on the dais under the unicorn tapestry. She waited for silence, gesturing to the men to remain seated. Then she spoke. "Gentlemen, today is Mayday, and, as you know, Mayday is ruled only by a queen. You have chosen me. Are you ready to obey my commands?" Some laughter, a murmur of amused consent. At a signal, a page brought out the rosewood box. Guenever continued, "I have an entertainment for you. A challenge, of a kind." She opened the box, and removed the horn. "Only he who has been faithful to his lady for the past year and a day may sound this horn. Come, gentlemen: let us hear your fidelity." Another murmur. "You agreed, did you not, that I had the right to command? Well, I command this to be done." She handed the horn to the page. "Take this to my knights, and let them essay this test."

I looked out into the chamber. The signs of discomfort were clear. Agravaine stared fixedly at his plate, red with embarrassment or, more likely, anger. Kay had his arms folded; his eyes narrowed as he watched the queen. Sagremore looked frankly terrified. Medraut was smiling; rising, he bowed and said, "Your majesty, if we have no lady?"

"Then you have nothing to fear," Guenever said. He shrugged and resumed his place.

The page reached the table and halted, looking up at the queen. She nodded, and he passed the horn to the first man. I looked sidelong at the other ladies. Andrivete frowned. Luned clutched her hands in her skirts, and muttered *sotto voce*. Alis was smiling. It seemed to me, abruptly, that we were taking a very great chance. Essyllt was thoughtless: she never looked beyond the moment. Andrivete was right: there was mischief in this. Too late, now, to stop it.

The horn passed from hand to hand. Young Alisander blushed as he sounded a note, high and true. Beside me, Alis clapped her hands in delight. Patrise next to him failed, and two more beyond him. Agravaine failed, and scowled at Laurel. Medraut drew one clear note and looked at us, laughing. "Does this mean," he said, "that I'm in love, and don't know it?" But after him, five successive failures. One of the ladies began, softly, to weep. Then a success, and another. Sagremore failed. The horn reached Kay, who held it for a moment, weighing it in his palms. He looked at Andrivete. "I can see, wife, that I'm going to have to increase your dress allowance." Laughter sprinkled the hall as he blew the horn, and played, albeit flat, the first few notes of 'Cuckolds All Awry'. Next to him was Gaheris, who did not look at the dais as the horn came to him. The note again was true. "You," said Luned, furiously, "you do this just to spite me. Do you think this makes you better than me?" He shook his head, and his eyes slid quickly from her face. After him came four more failures, a success, and another failure. It arrived at Gawain. He rose, and looked at the queen. "Is it worth my even trying?" He was laughing, but there was an air to him that bespoke disapproval.

"No exceptions, Sir Gawain," said the queen.

"Ah, well." He shrugged, and inhaled with exaggerated vigour. The horn made for him not the faintest sound. He shook his head, and handed it to Gareth.

Medraut said, "Unnecessary, surely. Is this not the very pelican of fidelity?" Gareth stopped and turned to look at him, the motion hiding his expression from me.

"Pelican?" someone said. And someone else answered "Thought that was for maternal devotion. He means swan."

"I said no exceptions," said the queen.

Gareth turned again, and looked up. Medraut had come to stand at his shoulder. Gawain moved to the very edge of the dais. I could almost touch him. Gareth raised the horn, hesitated, and looked at me. For a moment, it seemed he might speak. Then he closed his eyes, and blew.

There was no sound. For the longest moment I was waiting, expecting the note to rise. He was drawing his breath, that was all, in a second it would be over... No one moved, no one seemed even to breathe. Then Gareth lowered the horn. He opened his eyes, and looked at me again. Then he put his face into his hands.

There was a hand under my elbow. All around me, the ladies retreated. I could not look at their faces. Their hems rustled, brushing the rush matting; mud on one, a tiny tear in another... odd, what is noticed, what is forgotten. The hand slid up to my shoulder, and turned me with gentle ease.

"Llinos," Gawain said, softly, "Come and look at the rose garden."

# Three

"You knew," I said to him, on the terrace. A cool night had come in to follow the warm day: there were no clouds, and the moon was crisp and clear overhead. Gawain had draped his mantle over my shoulders: he held my hand in his as we sat on the low wall. "You knew. That's why you sent Medraut to me in Cornwall."

"I didn't know." With his free hand, Gawain brushed a speck of ash from his knee. "I suspected." He hesitated. "But I sent no one. I had no proof. And I have faith in Gareth."

"It's my fault, I stayed away…"

He shook his head. "It sounds shallow, but these things happen." A pause. "Gareth loves you."

I stared into the shadowy garden. "I shouldn't have come back."

I don't know precisely how long we stayed outside. Not long; no more, perhaps, than half an hour. I felt still, inside myself: my thoughts refused to move on from moment to moment. I was not ready to feel. It seemed that nothing would ever again reach me.

The corridors were empty when we went in. But lights burned under doors, and there was a continual murmur of voices. Most were hushed: in the painted chamber, they were raised. We could make out the words from the foot of the stair. The Orkneys. Always the Orkneys.

"...nonsense about pelicans!" That was Agravaine. He sounded disgusted.

"Believe it or not, Agrin, I was trying to help." Medraut, sounding irritated.

My Gareth's voice, then, softer, but still not low. "We know that, Mouse, but..."

"Will you stop calling me that!" Medraut snapped. Gawain and I were almost at the top of the stair. Through the open door, I could see Agravaine in the centre of the room, hands on hips, glaring. Medraut stood by the hearth, one elbow on the mantel; beyond him, Laurel hovered, twisting her veil. Gareth was out of my line of sight.

Agravaine drew in a long breath. "Yon test was false."

"Oh, aye." Medraut laughed without mirth. His eyes met mine briefly, as Gawain and I came into the room. Then they flickered to his eldest brother. "I'm sure Gavin will agree that he's the very zenith of virtue."

Gawain handed me to a chair. I could see the rest of them, now. Luned sat in the south window, spine rigid, face set. Gareth beside her avoided my gaze. Gaheris stood a little apart from the others, back to the room, staring through the other window into the night. Gawain found himself a corner of a chest, and sat down. Then he said "Like you, Mouse, I have no one to whom to be true."

"Don't call me that!" Medraut said again. And then "Not even a memory, Gavin?"

There was a nasty silence. No one ever talked about Gawain's long-dead Rhanillt; it was one of the family's unwritten rules. Medraut looked down. "I'm sorry. I didn't mean that."

"The Orkney talent," Gawain said. "Saying what we do not mean."

"I'd just like to know," Medraut said, "why you're all picking on me, when it was Gari who failed."

"We have no proof the test was true," Agravaine said stubbornly, drowning out an attempt to speak by Gareth, who shook his head and fell silent. "It was no more than women's meddling." Agravaine's eye fell on Laurel. "Aye, and a better test of female honesty than male. A true wife would not have let her husband go unwarned into such folly."

Laurel stared at her feet. "The queen made us swear…"

"The queen! Did God appoint the queen head over you, or your husband?" Agravaine took a step forward. "No, madam, this is more of your disobedience."

Laurel gave a little gasp. From the window, Gaheris said, "Let be, Agrin. Don't make this worse."

"You!" Agravaine was scornful. "You can't rule your own wife! Don't tell me how to treat mine."

"Our mother," Gawain said, "did not raise any of us to strike or bully a woman. Don't blame Laurel for your own bad temper."

Another silence. Then Luned said, lightly, "Well, your mother didn't do a very good job, did she?" Agravaine scowled. She smiled at him. "Just look what my husband did to *her.*"

Gaheris turned. He was white. "Is this my fault, now?"

"You shamed me before everyone," Luned said. "There's not a soul in this court believes there's more than air to our marriage. But you mock me with your sham fidelity."

"No, I…"

"Do you think that this will shrive you? Will these petty virtues wipe out what you've done?" Luned was trembling. "I live every day with your dishonour." Gareth reached out and put a hand on her arm. She ignored him. "Matricide and destroyer of good knights!"

Gaheris choked. He put a hand to his mouth, looking across at Gawain. Very carefully, Gawain said, "I am sorry for your pain, Luned, but it does no good to rehearse these matters."

"Why not?" Gareth said, suddenly. We all stared at him. "We never do talk about that, do we? Why is that, Gavin?" His voice was sharp, tight: still he would not meet my eyes. There was something here… Medraut had tried to warn me. *There has been something said, between Gareth and Gaheris.* Gareth swallowed. "Go on, Gavin, tell me."

"It hardly seems relevant…" Gawain said, but his voice was uncertain.

"The truth is," Agravaine said, "that Heris is your favourite. However clumsy he is, however stupid or vicious, you allow him anything."

Gawain looked up. "No, Agrin, I…"

"Listen to you!" Gareth interrupted him. "I want to talk about this now. I want to talk about Lamorak de Galis."

"What for?" said Agravaine. "Lamorak was no part of us. Son of our enemy, and despoiler of our mother. It's her death we should be thinking about."

Gareth ignored him, looking at Gawain. "Here you all are, gathered to rehearse my faults. But you called no family council over Heris."

"I called none over you." Gawain spoke softly, but in his voice was the leading edge of anger. "I took your wife from the sight of your shame, and I hoped to find you alone to receive her again." Laurel took a step forward, as if she would speak, then stopped at a glance from Agravaine. I pulled Gawain's cloak tighter about my shoulders, as though it might keep out the words.

Gareth released Luned's arm. I had almost never seen him angry. One thought of gentleness, of grace, in connection with him; easy enough to forget that he, too, was Margawse's son. Easy, until you caught sight of the tilt of his jaw, the line of his brow, the dark colouring in his eyes. An Orkney, every bit as much as the rest of them. He inhaled raggedly, and said, "Thank you, Gavin. May I point out to you yet another difference?" Gawain's eyes narrowed. I put out my hand, and Laurel took it. Gareth continued, "You interfere quite happily in my marriage. Yet you do nothing at all about Heris's."

I said, quickly, "It wasn't interference.", but no one paid any attention. There was a pause.

Then Gaheris said "If it helps, Gari, he's been nagging me for years."

"I don't believe you," Gareth said. "I don't see him sheltering your wife from your shame."

Gaheris looked down. Laurel said "But Heris didn't fail… If the test was true, he's loyal."

"I wish," Gaheris said, rather sharply, "you'd all stop talking about my character as if I wasn't here." He spread a hand out in front of him, and stared down at it. He looked cornered. "If you've something to say to me, Gari, say it, and have done."

"Loyalty," Gareth said, and stopped. For the first time since the test, he turned towards me. His face was quite blank, as if he was beyond any feeling save anger or confusion. A glance of a few seconds, no longer, then he looked away.

Into the silence, Luned said "Tell us about loyalty, Heris. How can you pretend to be loyal to me, when you couldn't keep faith with those for whom you actually cared? You broke faith with Lamorak. Why not with me?"

"I have no idea." Gaheris said. I tightened my hold on Laurel's hand. "I wasn't thinking." He sighed. "A year and a day… Chance. Does that help?"

"And Lamorak?" Gareth said. "He adored you. He named you his sponsor. He followed you everywhere, and you betrayed him." Gaheris let his head fall. Gareth said "You killed him."

"No!" Gawain, finally, had lost his temper. He came to his feet, glaring. "That's a lie. You will take it back, right now. Heris had no part in that death."

"Lamorak trusted him," Gareth said, simply.

"Aye," Gaheris looked up. "He trusted me, and it got him killed. You think I don't know that?" He came into the centre of the room. "I offered his brothers my life in return." He put a hand to his belt "The offer stands, Gari. I've a knife here, right now. You can use it, for Lamorak. Or," and he turned to Agravaine, "Agrin may, for mother." Agravaine stared at him, blankly. Gaheris swallowed, looked down at me. "I'm sorry, Llinos. All my fault. As usual."

No one moved. After a moment, Gaheris passed a hand across his eyes, looked down, and walked out. He didn't slam the door behind him.

Laurel had started crying. I could think of nothing to say to her.

Agravaine, surprisingly, seemed more puzzled than angry. Gareth stared at the floor. There was a long silence. Then Medraut stepped away from the hearth, and let a hand fall onto my shoulder. "Are you all right, Llinos?" I couldn't answer him. My mouth was too dry. He shook his head, then looked across at my sister.

"Well," he said, lightly, "are you happy, now? Have you got everything you wanted?" Luned flushed. "There's loyalty for you," he continued, "or don't you count it necessary, between sisters?"

Somehow, Medraut bundled them all out of the room, even Laurel, who wanted to stay. Luned had pulled down her veil: I think she wept behind it. Gawain kissed my cheek before leaving. "I should have known," he said, "I should have taken you to some more private place, and brought Gareth to you."

But Gareth would not speak to me. In the doorway, he paused, and looked back. "Llinos…" He shook his head, and fled. I had left him too long alone. I had lost him. I still couldn't feel it. I had lived so long with pain that I could not comprehend this new one. Medraut escorted me to my own room, and then, like Laurel, tried to linger. I sent him away. He sighed, ruefully, but he obeyed.

I couldn't sleep. I didn't even undress for bed. I sat in the window, chin on my knees, waiting for the dawn. Around me was only silence. I let the candles burn out, remained there in the dark. I sat there all night, but Gareth did not come.

# Four

A little after dawn, someone knocked on the door. It was Luned. She didn't look as if she had slept, either. She said "Is he here? I need to speak to him."

"Gareth? No."

I thought she would leave, then, but she hesitated, playing with the loose ends of her hair. She said "What do you want me to say? That I loved him first? It would be true." I said nothing. She wound her hair around her fingers, one way, another. I could remember that habit right back into our childhood. She said "You don't know what it's like, being married to Gaheris."

"Is that an excuse?"

"You're angry... I suppose that's fair. No one thinks you've done anything wrong. It's me that's the shrew, again. I've been so lonely." She looked away down the corridor. "I don't suppose you even want to hear this. Gaheris either ignores me or placates me. I don't love him. I never have, but..."

"Would you rather he abused you, as Agravaine does Laurel?"

"I don't know." She spoke slowly. "You can't imagine what it's like. Nothing I do touches him. Not even when I..." She stopped, then finished, "Not until now."

I could not be angry: the emotion was gone with the rest, buried under the grief. Yet something made me say "Is that why you did this to me? To get a reaction from Gaheris?"

"No." She looked back at me. "Not even I would do that. But Gareth saw, don't you see? He saw how unhappy I was, and he came to save me. And I didn't think about you at all, because you just didn't seem to need him any more."

I could hear the castle coming to life as I closed the door behind her. Someone else would come, all too soon. Laurel, or Andrivete, or kind Gawain. I had fled from their sympathy before. I could not bear to stay for it now: it would burn me. I gathered a few things into saddle bags. I'd leave orders that the rest be sent to me later. I'd be safe at Kinkenadron. I'd always been safe there. Only Gareth had ever broken through those walls. I'd held them secure two years against Ironside, the Red Knight of the Red Launds. I could hold them again. At home, I would know each and every one of my boundaries, and no one would hurt me again. I changed hurriedly into travelling clothes, and when my maid Alison came in, sent her to gather her own few necessities, while I fetched a day's rations. In less than an hour, we were ready. We were silent as we rode out of the stable yard and down towards the river. We would need no escort, not on the king's roads, along which it was said a maiden with a bag of gold might travel quite securely from one end of the kingdom to the other. It was better this way.

Alison and I were almost four miles from Camelot when we heard the sound of horses coming up fast behind us. Couriers, no doubt. Obedient to the regulation, we drew over to one side, and waited. Yes, there they were, two horsemen coming at the gallop down the hill. They wore no livery, though one had an indistinct badge on his shoulder. The morning air turned the leader's hair amber: for a breathless moment, I thought it might be Gareth.

Gareth was not so tall. I looked down, as the hoof-beats approached us, slowing to a walk. The horsemen reined in alongside us, and Alison bowed from the saddle. I turned. The leader pushed his hair back from his face with a large hand, and looked at me apologetically. The shoulder badge was his personal device, five long-stemmed flowers entwined in a pentangle: the rose knot. The same device was painted on the shield strapped to the saddle of the sleepy-eyed squire. I looked from one to the other. "Is something wrong? Is it Gareth?"

"No." Gaheris rested a hand on his saddle-bow. He wore travel gear: there were bags slung across his horse's rump. He shrugged. "Gavin sent me. To see you home." His expression was quizzical. "I think he wants me out of the way."

"Just you?" I said.

"Well, of course." Gaheris was puzzled.

It made no difference either way. I pressed my knees to my horse's sides, moving it to a walk. "So," I said, "let's go."

The weather was unkind. Day after day of clear skies and bright sun. All along the roads, trees blossomed; around their boles clustered the flowers of early spring. The nights were warm and balmy. We stayed in the houses of domain lords, as was the right of the king's knights, or with the dignitaries of the small towns. The officials talked to us of politics and taxes, trade and fashion and sheep. Everywhere I looked there were children: in the gardens of cottages, on village greens, in the houses and streets of the towns. And, too often, there were lovers of all kinds and conditions. It tore at me to see them. I felt very alone. We did not speak of what had passed, Gaheris and I. At first we exchanged only commonplaces, when we spoke at all.

After four days of travel, the settlements began to be further apart, the landscape wilder. On the western horizon, the dark smudge of Surluse forest grew. At a small manor, Gaheris bargained for a pack-horse, and a tent that was almost a pavilion. We would not venture into the forest, but we must pass close by it; we might not always be sure of lodging. Oh, to be sure, we might have avoided it wholly, turning north to take the Bristol pack-horse route. I had travelled that way in March, but it added ten days or more to the journey, and I longed to be home.

Our chosen route lay off the main roads: a track, even a path, unpaved, never pioneered by the distant Romans. It wound lazily, apt to the shape of the land, along shallow vales, skirting spurs, following the contours of hills. There were no orchards here, no nascent fields of corn. The ground grew stiff grass and gorse, and sheep wandered across it.

Hawthorn and scattered birch marked the leading edge of the forest; at night the wind brought the scent of bark and mulch. We camped by the path's side, close to rivulets, or in the lee of low hills. Gaheris and his squire, Evan, pitched the tent for Alison and me. They lay out under the sky. "What if it rains?" said Alison.

"We get wet," said Gaheris.

"His mail rusts, and I have to clean it," Evan finished gloomily.

But it did not rain. On the second day, we reached the border of the forest proper. Wide-spaced trees paced us, beech and ash and oak. There was grass and bracken beneath them: here, there was still sufficient soil and light. Deer and rabbit tracks wandered in and out; the sun patterned the leaves. Surluse seemed green and cool and inviting. All of us knew better than to wander in. We must skirt it for four more days, then turn south-west, towards the coast. The forest was content to ignore us; nothing came from it, apart from birds, and rabbits, and the occasional deer. Evan's skin turned brown from the sun, and Alison fussed with veils. Gaheris, as every year, began to freckle.

We forded two largish streams, and several minor ones. Gaheris kept a count, though I was uncertain why: the path was well-marked, and there were no junctions. Away from the vavasours and gentry, we began to talk to each other more. Alison flirted gently with Evan, or gossiped about the court. I heard about Evan's sister, who'd gone to a convent, not to take the veil but to learn surgery. "My mother would have approved," said Gaheris, then fell very silent.

Tacitly, we agreed not to discuss the condition of the family and the trouble we were in. Instead, I told over my plans for the home farm at Kinkenadron, or planned still room projects with Alison. I'd managed the household since my thirteenth year, when my father's sister left us to be married. My mother was long dead, and both Luned and I had grown up accustomed to help our aunt: the transition had seemed natural. When our father died, I took over management of the lands as well. I enjoyed it, and, moreover, found I had a gift for stewardship. It was only in martial matters that I had no grounding. I could neither lead nor muster men, and my illegitimate half-brother lacked both the age and the position to act in my stead. Yet with all this, Kinkenadron was no soft target. My ancestors had built it for strength, and I ran it to endure. When Ironside had besieged us, he had been unable to breach our walls, or starve us, or wrest away control. With our own water supply, and careful management, we'd been able to hold out until Luned brought us succour from Arthur's court.

Until Gareth arrived... How astonished he'd been to learn I was my own steward. But he was Margawse's son: he did not think such behaviour unfit. By marriage-law, my lands were now his, but he had not sought to overturn my dominion. I had thought it charmed him to have such a wife. He had always said as much.

And yet... Luned had accused me of not needing him. Perhaps I had been wrong all along. Perhaps I had been mistaken in believing he liked my independence. I had no answers, but I pondered as I rode.

Gaheris seldom ventured new topics of conversation, although he seemed willing enough to contribute to discussions of root vegetables and dyeing and bottling plums. He was surprisingly well-informed. When I asked, he shrugged. "It's the king, I suppose."

"The king?"

"The daily audiences. Either Kay or I have to attend him. The petitioners talk a lot about sheep and such."

"Yes, I suppose so."

"And then, Gavin…" He shook his head, abruptly, and stopped.

Family. It always came back to that, casting shadows over everything.

The third day beside the forest dawned cold and overcast. Evan squinted up at the sky and forecast rain with an air worthy of a septuagenarian, reducing the rest of us to laughter. We struck camp with greater than usual speed, and did not linger to break our fast. We had camped in a shallow coombe: the forest skirted us on more than half its circumference. The morning was very still: no birds sang. The path led up one side, narrow and flinty, then along a slight ridge, before beginning the slow incline downwards to the last ford. It was a river we must cross, rather than a stream, and one with a name for unreliability. It was, moreover, a boundary. Beyond it, the land no longer answered directly to Arthur, but rather to the rule of one of his sub-kings, my cousin Marcus, king of Cornwall. There had been talk, from time to time, of building a bridge, yet nothing ever came of it.

The border was ancient; even in these peaceful days there was a hesitance about compromising it.

We wound our way downhill in silence. Around mid-morning it started to drizzle, and I wrapped my cloak around me tightly. The horizon closed in: the hills were low and ragged. Beside us, the forest was dank and still. The change in weather had made Alison cross. She muttered to herself from time to time, frowning. Evan blew on his fingers, and made vain attempts to keep his face half dry. Gaheris kept looking into the wood. After a few miles he called a halt, and took his shield from Evan.

"What is it?" I asked. "Did you see something?"

"No." He hesitated. "I'm just jumpy."

It was a little before noon that it happened. The day had brightened, somewhat, and the drizzle had died away. Evan began whistling, tunelessly, between his teeth as he led the small party downhill. We had just crossed over another rivulet, which now ran parallel to us, bordering the forest. To the other side the land had become quite steep, and we were obliged to ride in single file. The path turned a corner. Evan headed round it, leading the pack-horse. Alison behind him. I had turned to ask Gaheris how much further we had to go, and wasn't paying especial attention to the path.

There was a sudden sharp crack, like ice, breaking. Gaheris yelled "Ware!" and spurred forward. I looked round wildly. Nothing, nothing… I'd dropped my reins. I leant forward, scrambling for them. Something struck me sharply on the back of the hand. I looked up. The hillside was moving.

No.

Earth and stone and even a bush or two, sliding downhill. I could feel the thrum of it underfoot. Pebbles bounced and tumbled past me. The larger rocks were slow, but gathering momentum. My horse twitched and shivered. The back of my hand stung. I made another grab for the reins.

Gaheris cannoned into the back of me. My horse shied. I made a wild grab for its mane. The horse threw up its head and leapt toward the water. Without the reins, I had no hope of halting it. I clung on. Water sprayed up around us. The horse started to canter. Up the far bank in a scrambling leap, and into the forest. Branches whipped past, snarling my hair and tearing my clothes. I lost my cloak. My eyes streamed and stung. Distantly, Gaheris yelled my name. I had no breath to answer. I hung on, and prayed the horse would stop. I could barely see where we were headed. We hurdled over a low clump of bushes: I banged my face on the horse's neck, and my nose started bleeding. I dared not raise a hand to staunch it. Gaheris' voice was gone. I could hear only wind, and hoof-beats. I could see nothing beyond blurred tree-shapes and thicket. The horse ducked and wove amidst them, taking us deeper and deeper into the forest.

I don't know how long we ran. I remember only speed, and chill, and bone-bruising jolting. We met a fallen bough, and the horse twisted beneath me. I lost my grip on the mane. The horse gathered itself to leap on further into the shadow. I made a grab for the pommel and missed. As the horse jumped, I slid forward, helplessly. I was falling… My head struck something hard.

Darkness and silence.

I awoke to a dull headache, and the smell of wood-smoke. Someone had spread a wool blanket over me, and under my head was a makeshift pillow. I opened my eyes to the grey light of evening, filtered through tree limbs. When I turned my head, I could see a small fire, and, beyond it, a tethered horse, and more trees.

No point, then, in asking where I was. This could only be the forest of Surluse. I started to sit, and a hand was placed gently on my shoulder. Turning the other way, I found myself looking directly at Gaheris.

He said, "How do you feel?"

"I'm not sure. I want to sit up."

He slid an arm under me, and helped. Then he said, "Can you see clearly? No blurring, or spots before your eyes?"

"No, they're all right."

"And you don't feel sick?"

"No. My head hurts, though."

"Aye." He was still supporting me with his arm. He shifted a little so that my head rested against his shoulder. "You've no bones broken, that I can tell. But I'm afraid I couldn't find your horse."

"I'm just glad you found me." He looked away, discomfited. "What do we do now?"

"We're stuck here for tonight, at least. I want to be sure you're all right." He glanced down at me again. "Evan has a good head on him: he'll have folk searching by now. Either

47

they'll come, or we'll bring ourselves out tomorrow." His voice was briskly certain. "Are you comfortable? I'm sorry I could do no better by you."

"It's not your fault, Heris."

But he didn't answer that.

It was another damp, chill morning. I was stiff from lying on the ground, but my head felt clear. I sat up, and stretched. The fire had gone out. A few feet away, Gaheris was asleep with his head on his saddle. He had neither cloak nor blanket: both had been wrapped around me. As I rose, he yawned and turned. We talked little as we struck our makeshift camp. I drank a few mouthfuls of water from his canteen, and used about an eggshell-full to wipe my face. Breakfast was half a slice of bread. Gaheris apologised twice for that, but I noticed that he ate nothing himself. He lifted me onto the back of his horse, and led us into the trees.

We pushed through thorn and bush, followed narrow deer tracks past immense oaks, ducked between scrub ash and birch. Birds called alarum at our passage, and rustled half-seen through the boughs. We couldn't see the sun, nor much of the sky. There was no sign anywhere of people. After a couple of hours, we came to a small stream. The water was brown and cold. The horse drank it thirstily. Gaheris, more cautious, would not let me drink until he had tasted it. "Muddy."

"But safe?"

"Who knows?"

Lunch was another half-slice of bread, a lump of cheese. Gaheris excused himself while I ate, and started us moving again on his return. By sunset, we had found nothing but thickets and more trees. As he lifted me down from the saddle, I said "Are we lost?"

"No," he said, shortly, and began to unsaddle the horse.

"Is there anything I can do?"

"You might find some fallen wood: we'll need a fire. Don't go too far away."

He'd insisted on that all day. Stay within earshot, better still within sight, even when in need of privacy. Turn your back, but stay close, within easy distance. Yes, and though he'd left his shield strapped to the saddle, he'd kept his sword to hand, and worn his mail. He watched the forest with wary eyes.

None but dark tales emerged from Surluse forest. Fell creatures, madmen, and treacherous faerie. My horse could hardly have taken me more than a few miles into it, yet here we still were. Something was wrong...

I gathered a double armful of twigs and small branches. They were damp: our fire would be a dismal affair. Gaheris finished untacking the horse, and spread the saddle blanket on the ground. He made me sit while he started the fire. It smoked and gave off little heat. He opened the saddle bags, and drank a mouthful of water before passing the canteen to me. He looked tired: his hair needed combing and mud streaked his face. Somehow, I doubted I looked much better.

He passed me an apple, then hesitated and did up the saddle bags. I said "Aren't you eating?"

"I ate before."

Over the years, I'd heard his fellows use a large number of epithets for his honesty. Every single one had been a variation on the extreme. The favourite tended to be one coined by Kay: crashingly. Gaheris's honesty even lay at the heart of this trouble over Lamorak and Margawse, for he had remained desperately, painfully silent, in the face of almost all questions. "You'd need to be stupid not to spot Heris lying," Luned had once said. "I've never known anyone so inept."

He was lying to me now. I put a hand on his arm. I said, "I don't think you did."

He flushed, looking at me sidelong. "Well, happen I forgot." I held his gaze. He shook his head, then gave me a quick, rueful, smile.

I said "How bad is it?"

"We have only what food I was carrying when your horse bolted. Not a lot." He looked down. "Still, it doesn't have to last long. We'll be out soon."

"Are you sure?"

"Well…" He laced his fingers. "We're not very lost. I know where we are to a degree. And I know any number of places where we aren't."

"Like Camelot, or Tintagel, or Carlisle?" I said, and he laughed.

"Aye. But we will be searched for. I'm certain of it."

"Will they find us?"

"Yes." He said. And then, "I think so. Gavin wouldn't give up. Nor your Gareth."

"If he is my Gareth, these days."

"He's always yours." Gaheris sounded unusually fierce. I gazed at him in some surprise. He blushed even more, but continued "It's my fault, this trouble you're in, not his."

"You said that before."

"Yes." He leant over, and prodded the fire. He said "What food we have might last through tomorrow. After that… I've no bow for hunting, but I know how to set snares, and I can live off the land, to a degree. I learnt that, campaigning. Happen we won't be comfortable, but we won't starve."

We wandered two more days, seeing nothing save trees and birds. It grew colder. I made Gaheris take back his cloak, but it was too cold to sleep. My bones ached, and my hands grew chapped and sore. I made sporadic attempts to tidy myself, but my hair snarled in Gaheris' small comb, and my over-dress was stained and torn. Gaheris looked tired under the dirt, and his beard was growing raggedly. Meals were erratic and basic. Of the three of us, the horse fared the best, for there was some greenery suitable for it to eat, and it seemed to suffer less from the cold. The third day differed somewhat from the preceding two: it began to rain. That evening, we couldn't start a fire at all, and perforce went colder still and hungry. Gaheris looked at me, shivering under the blanket, and swore. Then he apologised, and unbelted his sword: that night we shared the covers, the blade naked between us. There were more days after that, and more nights: I don't remember how many. Once, a white deer bounded across the path before us. I stared after it dully, while Gaheris crossed himself.

I said "We should follow it."

"How?" he said. "The horse would break a leg in those thickets."

Perhaps that was the first day I saw the knight in grey, I'm not sure. I recall the slow sensation of being watched growing over me with the passing hours. And then looking into the trees to see an indistinct shape hovering several yards away, beside a tall birch. I turned to tell Gaheris: when I looked back, it was gone. After that, I saw it several times a day, although never clearly, never close. Gaheris saw nothing. He thought I was hallucinating, I could tell, though he went out of his way not to comment.

He still swore that someone, sooner or later, would find us. I was less sure. If Gareth no longer loved me, if he loved my sister... He would never deliberately harm me, nor act maliciously. But perhaps he would not hunt too hard. I would have such thoughts late in the night, cold and uncomfortable on the damp ground, and be shamed by the memory come morning.

There came a time when nothing was caught in Gaheris's snares, when we could find no early berries, no roots, no stored nuts. We were deep inside the forest, surrounded by oaks so vast they might have been growing in Abraham's time. The ground was barren: mud and dead leaves. The horse plodded along with sunken head, suffering now as we did from hunger. It rained more or less continuously: I could not remember exactly what warmth had felt like. And I was so tired, I kept falling asleep on horseback, and Gaheris kept waking me up again. When I opened my eyes, black spots swam before them. The knight in grey was riding parallel to us: I waved to him, and smiled. He bowed to me from the saddle. "There," I said to Gaheris, "you were right. They've found us."

"You have to stay awake," Gaheris said.

We were following another deer path. After a while, it forked, and Gaheris made to turn right. The knight in grey stood beside the other branch. I looked at him, and he beckoned. "No," I said to Gaheris, "The other way."

He looked at me oddly. I picked up the reins to turn the horse. I said "We have to go left." Gaheris shrugged, and led us that way. The track wandered under the trees, narrow and winding, and the knight in grey paced us in silence. It began to grow dark, and Gaheris wanted to look for somewhere to camp. I shook my head at him. We skirted trees and picked our way among fallen branches. "We must stop soon," Gaheris said, "There'll be an injury, if we go on much longer. It's too dark."

"Not yet," I said. The knight in grey nodded to me, approving. We went on along the path as night came in. The rain slackened to a fine drizzle. I could barely see my hand on the pommel, but the knight in grey was clear before me, glowing with his own faint light. We plodded on in silence.

The path seemed wider and smoother. The trees were spacing out.

Gaheris said "What's that?"

I peered into the gloom. He was pointing forward, past the knight in grey, at a dim pale smudge. I said, "I don't know." We moved on towards it. Gaheris drew his sword, holding it in front of him. I could hear something, water flowing ahead...

The path came to an end. The knight in grey halted and pointed. There was a small glade, edges indistinct. The sound of water perhaps attested to a small stream bisecting it. In the centre of the glade stood a square white pavilion, lit from within. From its flag-pole a pennant flew, device invisible against the night sky. Gaheris called out "Hello?" There was no reply. He released the bridle. "Wait here," he said to me. Then he crossed to the pavilion, and went in.

I looked at the knight in grey. He nodded once, and faded back into the wood. Gaheris came out of the pavilion. "There's food, and a fire, and candles, but no people. It's probably a trap."

"I don't care," I said, dismounting. "I'm so hungry."

"Aye," Gaheris said, "but..."

"It could be months before we're found, or find our own way out," I said. "It could be never."

"I don't want your blood on my hands, too."

"I don't want to die of cold in the forest."

We looked at each other in silence. Then he sighed, and said, "As you wish, then."

Inside the pavilion stood a low table spread with food and drink: fresh bread, roast meats, cheese, apples, honey. The wine was warm and spiced. On a stand to one side stood a bowl of heated water, and soap, and towels. Candles burned in tall silver stands. A fire burnt in a neat stone pit. There were piles of cushions, worked in silk and brocade. Against the sides were two cots, made up with thick blankets and linen sheets. In a sack by the door were oats for the horse.

"Someone was expecting us," Gaheris said.

He insisted on seeing to the horse while I washed. The water was scented, and stayed clear, even when I washed my hair. There was a small hand mirror beside the basin, and I sighed over the state of my gown. Small chests stood at the foot of both the cots: on an impulse, I opened one of them. A shift, worked in green at neck and cuff, and a russet over-gown. I changed, rolling my soiled garments into a heap, and pushing them into a corner. When Gaheris came back in, I was brushing out my hair. He said "There's an enclosure, out there, laid out as a stall..." Then he noticed my clothes.

"I think the owner won't mind the loan."

"I've always liked that colour." He hesitated. "I'd forgotten how pretty you are." Then he blushed scarlet, and looked at his feet. "I'm sorry. I never could govern my tongue."

"Do you still think this is a trap?" I asked him.

"I don't know." Unexpectedly, he grinned. "If so, it's a rare fine one. "

He wouldn't let me go outside while he washed and changed. I sat on the end of one of the cots with my back turned. I felt unreasonably calm and happy, as if I'd finally found sanctuary from all my pain. I think Gaheris may have felt much the same way: when he came to hand me to table, he was smiling.

Despite the time we'd taken, washing and tidying, the wine was still warm in the jug and the roast meats hot. The taste of it all was splendid. I think I ate my fill, yet the table seemed scarcely depleted. There was an enchantment here, for sure. Licking honey off my fingers, I noticed that Gaheris had started frowning.

"What is it?" I asked.

"Nothing… I'm wondering if there's to be a price. I mind what happened to Gavin, years back…" He stopped, suddenly, and drank another mouthful of wine. "Well, I'll be the one to pay it. I owe you that."

I was warm, and full, and perhaps a little drunk. I said, "You keep saying that. But I don't see how any of this can be your fault."

"I should have insisted we took the long way round the forest."

"You were blaming yourself before that." I drew in a deep breath. "You blamed yourself the night of the test." He looked down. "Why, Heris?"

"Because it's true."

"Is it?" I ran a finger along the rim of my wine cup. "Did you force Gareth to be unfaithful?" Gaheris made no answer. "Tell me what happened."

He rose, and went to the flap of the pavilion, lifting it to look out into the night. After a while, he said "I don't know, precisely. Gareth and I quarrelled. That's all."

"What about?" He was silent. "About Lamorak de Galis?"

Gaheris inhaled. "Yes. About Lamorak."

"Tell me," I said.

"I don't know if I can." He looked down. There was another long silence. Outside, it seemed to be raining again. Gaheris dropped the flap and came back to the table, where he poured himself more wine. Then he said, "Gareth thinks it's my fault Lamorak died."

"So I gathered. But you didn't kill him."

"I'm not sure." Gaheris stared into his cup. I looked across at him in surprise. Glancing up, he met my eyes, and shrugged. "Oh, I didn't strike the fatal blow. But I misjudged some things." I watched him without speaking. "I botched the business with mother. So Agrin and Mouse went off after him."

"And Gareth thinks you should have stopped them?"

"Gareth," said Gaheris, "thinks I shifted the blame for mother's death from myself to Lamorak." His tone was utterly flat. Something in the line of him hinted at the famous Orkney temper. He shook his head. "I expect Gavin would say that was irony."

It took me a few moments to work that one out. Then I said, carefully, "Are you saying that Lamorak killed Margawse?" He was silent: his eyes slid away from mine. "Heris?"

"It isn't important any more."

"It is to me."

He swallowed more wine. "Gari's strong on honour. Upholding it. He thinks I failed. He feels sorry for Luned, because she's tied to me." He hesitated. "And he likes to rescue people. My fault. I'm sorry. Agrin has always said I'm stupid."

I said "But it was you who offered blood reparation to Lamorak's brothers."

"Hypocrisy. Or bad conscience." Again, that flat tone, that shadowing of anger.

"According to Gareth?" I said.

"You mustn't blame him." Gaheris put his cup down, and leant towards me. "He's right. Lamorak died because of me. Because I…" And he stopped, abruptly, and looked away. "It was an accident, my mother's death. Lamorak had had an *affaire* with her, but I meddled, and he tried to break it off. She attacked him, knifed him, and he pushed her away. The fall broke her neck." He swallowed. "When I found them, all I could think of was getting him away before the others found out. I thought I could take it on myself… I told Lamorak to go away and stay away. He didn't listen." He halted, briefly, studying his hands. "Agrin found out about the *affaire,* and decided that that was grounds enough. When Lamorak came back… I'd no way of warning him. Oh, Gavin wanted to fight him fair, but the others… They had to have a scapegoat, you see. Couldn't soil their hands with a brother's blood." He looked across at me again. "You see: I messed up."

Slowly, I said "Does Gareth know what happened? Exactly, I mean."

He shook his head. "Why haven't you told him."

"I've never told anyone, till now. The way Gari feels about me, he wouldn't believe me anyway. And there's no point to it. Lamorak's name has suffered enough. He was my friend."

"What about your name?"

"Doesn't matter."

"Heris," I said, "this is a mess."

"Aye." Unexpectedly, he smiled. "I've a rare talent for them. And for growing maudlin in my cups."

"Do you think we'll ever find a way out of this forest?"

"Yes." He rose. "It's late. We should sleep."

I rose in turn and smiled at him. There was wine warm within me, and light and shelter where there had formerly been only cold and confusion. I was safe, safe… It was the wine, perhaps, that gave me courage, but it was the sense of security which led me to stand on tiptoe and kiss him, once, very lightly, on the lips. "Good night, Heris."

"Good night."

I awoke clear-headed and warm. Sunlight filtered in through the sides of the pavilion. The blankets were thick and real over me. But for the rest... I rubbed my eyes, sitting up, uncertain if I was yet fully awake. The canvas was old and stained: lichens grew on it in patches. The cushions were rotted through, discoloured and damp. There were no candles, no dishes, no bowls. The table had lost a leg, and lay mildewed at a rakish angle. My original clothing lay folded over one of the chests, clean and neatly mended. Across the pavilion, Gaheris's mail coat had been buffed and cleaned. Our one set of saddle bags appeared now to be full to bursting. I crossed myself. Then I pulled my kirtle over my shift and set about rising. There was still water in the ewer, and it was clean, although cold. On one of the stools rested a loaf of new bread, a flagon of ale, and a large wedge of cheese. I finished dressing, then prodded Gaheris with a finger.

He sat up, and looked. I said, "What happened?"

"I don't know. Some kind of magic." He frowned. "We'd best move on. Could be dangerous to overstay our welcome."

Over his protests, I went out to tack up the horse, while he washed and dressed. The pavilion was as worn from the outside as it seemed from within. It stood in a small glade, with moss underfoot, tall old trees round about, and a small stream crossing one corner. There was no sign of my guiding knight in grey. The sun was up: today we would go dry.

The horse seemed as rested as I was, although the stall had overnight transformed into a tethering post and a rusted bucket. There were still oats at the bottom, and they were fresh and good. The tack had been cleaned and mended, like everything else. I saddled and bridled the horse quickly, then led it round to the front.

Gaheris came out of the pavilion with the saddle bags. "Enough food for a week," he said, "For the horse, too. Plus what we've been left for this morning, and the blankets, and a second cloak."

"We've been well looked after, here."

"Aye. God be thanked." He crossed himself.

We ate and made ready to leave. Gaheris, superstitious like all his kin, paused to pour a few drops of ale on the threshold. Then he looked up, and his face went utterly still.

"What is it?" I followed his gaze upward, to the tattered pennant which still fluttered over the pavilion. It had once been white, perhaps, and the device worked on it in red and green and brown. A snake, coiled up the stem of a single flower.

I knew it, of course. The serpent rose. Lamorak de Galis' personal badge.

We didn't talk much, that day. Gaheris was preoccupied, struggling, perhaps, with his old demons. The open glade and clear weather had given us a chance to guess approximate directions, and around noon I climbed a tree to confirm them. Gaheris was surprised at that. I smiled. Luned isn't the only tomboy in my family. I tried, a time or two, to tell him of the knight in grey, but it soon became clear that the subject distressed him. It seemed our lives would never be disentangled from the matter of Lamorak. Lamorak had died somewhere in this forest, at Orkney hands. Perhaps our pavilion had been his last living home: both of us, I think, thought so. Neither said it. And then there were the ghost tales. Yet, if ghost indeed it was, it seemed kindly disposed to us. Something of the safety I had felt in the pavilion travelled with me still. It seemed I had been running away from my bereavement and confusion, deep into this forest. But now I was ready to move on. Neither my lost daughter nor my cracked marriage were forgotten, but I had remembered something else. Once, I had possessed the strength to rule my own lands and hold out against all comers; the strength to be myself, independent, intact. I had found that again.

We slept dry, that night, if outdoors, and I awoke to find Gaheris's arm about my shoulders, despite the sword between us. I was still safe. It was another warm day, and we made good progress in a direction which we both considered to be south west. The forest around us had started to change. Dark, close-packed, heavy oak gave way to wider-spaced beech and sycamore and chestnut. Underfoot was low bracken, and sometimes grass. We passed through glades of bluebells, startling birds and small beasts. Amidst the trees, deer cropped shoots, and watched us with wary, liquid eyes. In a small clearing we came to a spring, surrounded by worked stone, and with a cross carved above it. The water was clear and cool in my cupped palms. It tasted sweet. Gaheris, as ever, hesitated to drink, yet followed me. This was more like the forest I remembered of old, filled less with shadow than with mystery. I rode without a veil, and with my cloak rolled behind me. I would be as brown as any farm girl. I felt young, and very free.

Something had changed. When Gaheris helped me dismount that evening, I lingered with his big hands still on my waist, and said "You always do this. I could get down alone."

"Aye," he said. And then "It is a habit I have from Gavin. He calls it courtesy." He smiled as he spoke, and there was a glimmer of laughter in his voice.

We were very close. His hands still steadying me, one of mine on his shoulder. I could feel his breath on my hair. He added "Do you mind?"

"No," I said, looking up at him. "I like it."

We were merry over our small fire, and from time to time our hands touched, passing the flask, the bread, the knife. I liked that, too. I remembered Essyllt, creamy in the tower room, so long ago. I was seeing Gaheris through her eyes. I did not think about Gareth at all. And when Gaheris made to lay the sword between us, I put my hand over his, and shook my head.

"I wonder," he said, as his arms came around me, "if we should not have drunk from that spring?"

My hands tangled in his hair, found the shape of jaw and throat. I said, indistinctly, "I have no idea." I kissed him. "Are you saying we should stop?"

He kissed my neck, and his hands made a start on my lacings. "Very probably", he said, good-naturedly. "What do you think?"

"Umm." Another kiss. "Don't know. Maybe later…"

Later, there was laughter. I propped myself on my elbows, and looked down at Gaheris as he laughed and laughed, spluttering somewhat as my hair got into his mouth.

"What is it?" I demanded.

"Nothing." He was breathless. "I was just thinking… Gavin sets such a bad example."

For some reason, that struck me as funny, too.

# Five

That was our last night in the forest, and we lingered over it, unknowing. We rose leisurely, and late, and lost more time playing over breakfast. The horse was patient with us, cropping grass, and refraining from looking resigned. It took me three attempts to mount. I kept being distracted, Gaheris's hands on my waist, his strength, his warmth… The sun shone bright around us and birds sang, it seemed, in every tree. We idled our way along the deer paths. Perhaps that was itself some part of the enchantment of this place, that it drew us out of all sense of responsibility.

Around mid-afternoon, we came to another glade, and a stream. The latter ran wide and fast-flowing, with a stone causeway laid athwart the narrowest part. On the nearer side stood a pavilion of weathered green; above this flew a pennant of plain white cloth. Gaheris and I looked at each other, and he put a hand to the hilt of his sword.

The tent flap lifted, and a man stepped out. He wore blackened mail, without surcoat or sash. His bucket helm had no crest, and hid his face entirely. There was no device upon his shield. His voice, when he spoke, sounded muffled and strange, even though his words held no surprise at all. He seemed to look us up and down. Then he said, "I am the guardian of this ford. None shall pass, save they win the right by force of arms."

"Fair enough," said Gaheris. "The terms?" And then, straightening a little, "I mean, I accept your challenge, sir knight," He was not quite taking the situation seriously: nor was I, come to that, light-headed on sunshine.

"I have not," said the stranger, "made you a challenge." There was a small pause. "I do not fight with churls."

Gaheris is as much an Orkney as any of his brothers. His chin came up, at that. But he said only "No more do I. Your terms?"

The dark figure regarded us in silence for a long moment. "A serjeant run away with his master's horse and arms? And mayhap his master's lady, too. I will take all three from you, and leave you grateful for your life."

"Oh, will you?" Gaheris said, sounding very like Gawain. "I'll take your terms, Sir Arrogance, and we'll see who's the churl."

"Then arm yourself," the stranger said. I kept my eyes on him as Gaheris unslung his shield and adjusted his mail: he had no helm, lost somewhere in our descent into the forest. As he turned to tie back his hair with a thong, he touched my arm. "I'm sorry about this."

"Not your fault, surely?"

"If I looked less disreputable… If he shows any sign of beating me, you're to put my horse to the gallop, and get away across the ford before he can lay hands on you."

"And leave you to face his annoyance?"

"Yes." Gaheris turned back to face the stranger, and drew his blade. They advanced to meet each other in the centre of the glade. Both moved warily, circling, trying to gauge the other's worth. Gaheris was the taller and heavier, but the stranger seemed quicker on his feet. The first two or three blows were almost perfunctory, aimed to test rather than damage. Then the stranger let out a yell, feinted low, and aimed a cut up under Gaheris's shield. Gaheris twisted left, catching the edge of the blow on the rim of his shield. The stranger pulled back and cut high, in time to deflect a blow himself. A flank cut, and Gaheris chopped down with his shield, slashing at the stranger's arm. Around us, birds cried alarum and fled away into the wood. Blow followed blow, loud and incongruous in the sleepy sunlight. Inch by inch, Gaheris, fighting defensively, gave ground. His face was set, eyes intent on the stranger, oblivious to all around. A twisting cross-body cut caught under his guard: blood dripped from his forearm. The stranger used his own shield almost like a second weapon, charging Gaheris's sword, seeking to shunt it aside. It was a style of fighting I remembered from somewhere before.

The stranger aimed another blow high, then pulled back before it could connect. Wrong-footed, Gaheris made an awkward parry, leaving his left side open. I watched the sword striking down, glittering wickedly in the sun. Gaheris lunged across himself in desperate motion, and drove the rim of his shield into the stranger's mid-section. The sword-cut connected with his shoulder, and skidded off his mail. The stranger pulled back again, gasping, and Gaheris brought the edge of the shield up in a sweeping body-blow, with all his considerable weight behind it. He followed it with a solid strike to the stranger's knee with the flat of his blade. The stranger dropped.

Gaheris put a foot on his sword-wrist, and levelled his blade at the eye-slit of the helm. There was a short silence. The stranger let his sword drop. Then he said, in a different tone, "All right, I yield. Can I get up now?"

"You're still a bloody maniac." Gaheris sounded furious: I looked at him in surprise. He was flushed; his eyes were narrow and intent.

"Indubitably." One-handed, the stranger was struggling to release his shield. He wasn't making a very good job of it. "But I should like to get up."

Gaheris muttered something inaudible, and stepped back. The stranger sat up, removed his shield, and rubbed the wrist which had been stepped on. "You weigh too much," he said, conversationally. Gaheris made no reply. The stranger climbed to his feet, and pulled off his helm.

Safere the Moor, Palomides' brother, and one of the companions of the Round Table. I must have looked surprised, for he caught my eye, and made me a small bow.

"Churl, am I?" said Gaheris. And then, "You're supposed to be in Gaul."

"I became bored. Gaul isn't very interesting unless one has Claudas' favour." Safere went back to rubbing his wrist. "I see, king's son of Orkney, that you still desire to break my bones."

"You were supposed to keep Lamorak in Gaul."

"You were supposed to protect him from your charming brothers, beautiful Gaheris." There was a long silence. Gaheris looked down. Then Safere said, silkily, "But Little Snake was wilful. He never would do what I told him."

Gaheris said "You can hate me all you want. But there was a lady's honour threatened here." Safere spread his hands, and smiled. Gaheris looked across at him, and added, "And for no reason I can think of. You'd hardly have a use for her."

The Orkney brothers have enemies in the most unexpected places. I inhaled, wondering if Safere would renew the fight. But he only shook his head, and started laughing. "Granted. But I could always have escorted her back to her husband. You're headed in quite the wrong direction for Arthur's lands, you know."

I said "We're on our way to my estate at Kinkenadron."

Safere looked across at me, speculatively. "All unchaperoned? Irregular, surely, even for the Orkney clan."

"Shut up," Gaheris said, through clenched teeth.

"Or you'll make me?" Safere smiled. "I'm certain we've had this conversation before."

"We lost our companions in the forest," I said. "If you know a way out, I'd be grateful if you'd direct us."

Safere glanced at Gaheris, who looked away. "As it happens, it's for that reason that I put myself in your way. *Your* safety," and he made me another bow, "has never been in doubt."

Gaheris said "What exactly are you up to?" But Safere only smiled again, and shook his head.

Within two hours, we were at the edge of the forest. Flower-spattered meadow ran away before us down to an earthen road. A party of riders made their leisurely way along it, accompanied by fluttering bright pennants and a distant sound of music and laughter. Safere nodded once to me, and faded back into the trees. I looked at Gaheris. "What was all that about?"

"Lamorak." Gaheris looked away. Then he looked back, and smiled. "Let's go."

Half-way down the meadow, the riders caught sight of us, and halted. Several waved: as we drew nearer, a couple of them rode forward to meet us.

It was my cousin by marriage, Essyllt, the queen of Cornwall. She embraced me, warm and perfumed, and smiled at Gaheris. "My goodness," she said, laughing as ever, "just look at you! Whatever happened?"

"We got lost," I said.

"Oh, that horrid forest!" She hugged me again. "Well, you're safe now, lovey. You shall come and stay with me."

Later, bathed and changed and well fed, I curled up in the window seat of her luxurious solar, and told her the whole long tale. Her lovely eyes filled with tears when I related the part about Gareth and Luned. She said "Oh, but it's all my fault. That ridiculous horn."

"No. I'm glad I know, It's better. And other people knew before. They tried to warn me. Medraut, for one."

She let it pass, shivering in delicious, vicarious horror at our experiences in the forest. When I came to the part about the night after we found the spring, I blushed, and fell silent.

Essyllt clapped her hands. "There!" she said, "Revenge is sweet, isn't it?"

I had been gazing into my lap: I looked up. "It wasn't revenge. I didn't even think about Gareth. It was just… Gaheris thought it might be some spell in the springwater."

"And," she prompted, "was it?"

"No, I don't think so. I just wanted to, just for myself."

She crossed the solar, and sat down beside me. "And now?"

"It won't happen again," I said, confidently.

I suppose I could easily have travelled on to Kinkenadron from Essyllt's summer palace, but she urged me to stay. She kept a warm, welcoming, informal court; it was simple to sink into it. Gaheris, I think, would have left had Tristan been there, but the Cornish champion was away in the north. Dinadan was there, and Gauter; and Essyllt's complacent husband, my cousin Marcus, stopped by from time to time, when his duties brought him to the neighbourhood. I'm fond of Marcus. He'd been kind to me and mine, even though he'd been unable to prevent Ironside's siege of my lands. I felt comfortable and at home, surrounded by friends who offered no pity and expected nothing. I felt young again.

Gaheris and I did not speak of what had transpired in the forest, although we spent a great deal of time in each other's company. He seemed happy, too, and I wondered if he had also escaped the clutches of old grief and trouble. No one spoke of Lamorak, any more than of my lost child, or of faithless Gareth. "How indolent we are," I said to Gaheris one afternoon, as we wandered in Essyllt's rose garden.

He shrugged. "It suits you. You're prettier than ever." Then he blushed and hastily began to talk about horses.

I think I might have slid gradually into staying there forever. I had neither need nor reason to leave. From time to time Gaheris expressed concern over the whereabouts of Alison and Evan, or wondered if he should let his brothers know of our location, but as far as I know he took no steps concerning either. The rest of June passed us by, and July began: it would soon be time for the harvest. I laughed, and danced, and played with Essyllt's courtiers by day, and at night slept without dreams.

Around the beginning of August, I realised that Essyllt was once again up to something. She'd been conducting a superficial flirtation with a young knight from West Cornwall, but the indications were that it was starting to pall. Marcus, indulgent, proposed summoning a tourney to amuse her, but she pouted, and complained she would have no champion. The next day, she started making up to Gaheris.

We were on the south terrace. Essyllt had had her chair carried inside, and reclined instead on a pile of cushions. I was perched on a low wall, engaged on a piece of embroidery. Dinadan for some reason was lying at my feet and getting in the way. Amant, the current favourite, had begun picking at a lute, but Essyllt abruptly frowned, and waved him away. "I'm tired of music. I want someone to read to me." She looked around at the assembled company. "Prince Gaheris?"

Gaheris had been conducting a low-voiced unromantic conversation with Brangwen about bee-keeping. He looked up, startled, as Essyllt beckoned him over. He didn't read aloud at all well: his voice was a steady monotone, and he stumbled over the longer words. Gawain would have made a pretty game of it, smiling at the queen as if the words were written for her alone. Gaheris appeared to be feeling picked on. "Oh, dear," murmured Dinadan to me, "another lamb to the slaughter."

"Gaheris has more sense," I said, and surprised myself with my own vehemence.

Essyllt insisted on keeping Gaheris by her for the rest of the day, and all of the next. By supper-time on the second evening, I was fuming.

It was, of course, thoroughly irrational. I didn't wholly understand it myself. My sister had taken Gareth from me, and I had been powerless. Some reprehensible part of me was determined to win this lesser match, perhaps from sheer spite. After the meal, Essyllt called for dancing. When the figure brought us together, I caught Gaheris' arm, and said "Take me outside."

He looked perplexed, but obeyed. Out in the courtyard, he said anxiously "Are you ill? Shall I call one of the maids?"

"No... It was a little hot in there." Essyllt might soon start wondering where we were. I drew him across the courtyard, and into one of the tack-rooms. "I wanted to talk to you."

"Of course." He handed me to the single stool, then leant against the wall. "What is it? Is it Gareth?"

"No," I said, before I could think too hard about that. And then, "Do you like the queen of Cornwall?" He shrugged. "She's making it plain she likes you."

His face cleared. "It's all right, Llinos. Agrin has it I'm stupid, but I'm not that stupid. She's my host's wife. And then, I'm not over-fond of Tristan's temper. I was Gawain's squire long enough to know how to duck if I have to." He smiled. "You mustn't worry."

"I wasn't." I looked at him, big and pragmatic and straightforward. "Heris, were you ever in love?"

"I don't think so." He considered the question for a moment. "Not really. "

"You're too sensible."

"Perhaps." He studied the back of his hands. "Or perhaps I'm just too dull."

"You always do that," I said. "You're your own worst critic."

"Aye, so Gavin tells me."

He wasn't looking at me. I rose, and went to stand before him. "Heris?" When he didn't reply, I put my hand against his cheek. "I wish you wouldn't be so hard on yourself. I don't find you dull or stupid. I think you're lovely."

He inhaled sharply, then he caught at my hand. "Llinos, don't."

"Why not?"

He shook his head. "A lot of reasons."

"So?"

"It is adultery. And incest. A sin." He swallowed, and looked down. "Because revenge is a poor reason, that hurts the avenger as much as the target."

I said, "I don't want you to make love to Essyllt." I'd started to cry, silently. He looked up, at that moment, and saw the tears.

He said "I'm not intending to."

"She gets what she wants. Like Luned."

Gaheris cursed. For an instant, I thought he would turn away. I said, quickly, "Don't leave me," and his brows drew in, worried.

He said "What can I do?"

"Hold me."

He hesitated. I swallowed, and added, "Please." He shook his head again, but his arms came around me. I leant my forehead against his shoulder, and put my own arms about his waist. Warm, and solid, and strong.

After a moment, he began to stroke my hair. Very softly, he said "This is no good."

"I know." But neither of us let go. I said "That spring, in the forest…"

"That was an excuse," Gaheris said. I looked up at him, and he smiled.

I said "The sin is already committed, then."

"We do not have to make it worse."

"Heris, I'm tired of being good."

"Aye."

We looked at each other in silence for a while. Then he said, carefully, "Once could be excused, I think. Especially in those circumstances. But twice…" He paused, and drew in a long breath. "It isn't that I don't want to. You're beautiful. I've always thought so. But Gareth loves you more than his life."

"That didn't stop him sleeping with my sister." And Luned would have had none of Gaheris's scruples. My throat was tight. I was shaking. "I can't do it any more. I can't just be Gareth's wife. I lost his child, and I lost him: all I have left is myself." My voice rose. He put a finger to my lips.

He said "Gareth is in hell without you."

"Then he should never have done as he did."

"Oh, sweet Jesu." Gaheris closed his eyes. "I'm no good for you. I'm no good at complicated things."

"This isn't complicated."

"It will be." He opened his eyes again. "I told you: I have a talent for getting into messes." He looked away from me, and his face was troubled. He had his own demons, as I had mine.

Some burdens are lighter when shared. I reached up and turned his face back towards me. "Heris, I don't care."

He gazed at me for the longest while. Then his arms tightened about me, and his mouth found mine.

He was right about the complications. Even in Essyllt's relaxed court it was not easy to carry on an illicit liaison. And then, I had no experience in subterfuge. Within two days, I think, most of the company was aware that something was going on. Essyllt herself took it well, kissing me, and whispering, "Never again?" with a wicked light in her eyes. But once commenced, I had no desire to stop. Gaheris came to my chamber late at night, or in the early afternoon, when most of the court rested. We met in the rose garden, in the hay- loft, behind the dovecots. I suppose we were not in love, but there was a great deal of affection between us, and a great deal of passion. I was beginning, at last, to understand Essyllt.

I was also beginning to understand Gareth. My loneliness craved the comfort and consolation of Gaheris, and I had chosen seclusion in the first place. How much more necessary such reassurance must have seemed to Gareth, abandoned at court, and vulnerable to love-hungry Luned. I said as much to Gaheris, He looked at me thoughtfully, and said, "Luned has made him very unhappy."

"And you?"

"I don't love my wife. It wouldn't be fair of me to be jealous." He kissed my fingers. "I'm angry at the hurt to you and Gari."

"Did you know?" I asked him, remembering our conversation on Mayday.

He shook his head. "I knew she had a lover, but I was not certain who… Gareth wasn't the first, you see: there have been several. Lamorak, for one."

"And you don't mind?"

"About Lamorak, or about Luned?" His tone was curiously wary. I looked at him. He said "It has been said that I killed my mother for jealousy over Lamorak."

"But you didn't kill her at all."

"No."

This was dangerous ground. Very carefully, I said, "Who said that?"

He turned his face away. "People. Agrin."

Here was another of those dark currents which ran through the Orkney clan. I stroked his hair. There was something vulnerable about Gaheris, for all his size. He did not know how to defend himself. I said, "You let your brothers bully you."

"Aye." He turned again, and his lips twisted a little, self-mocking. "Gavin tells me so at regular intervals. Loudly, usually."

I laughed at that, and kissed him. "Your family is so involved with itself. That isn't all bad. You and Gawain have been very kind to me. And Medraut tried to warn me about Gareth and Luned, months back."

"Oh, Mouse has trouble with his conscience." Gaheris' voice was abruptly absolutely flat. I'd learnt to recognise that tone. It signalled pain. He added "Mouse would feel badly

about hurting *you*. You're guiltless, by his lights. Whereas I...
He didn't give a tuppenny damn about Gareth's anger. But
Gareth and Luned..."

"Heris," I said, "what are you talking about?"

"Lamorak. As usual."

"But why should Medraut feel badly..." I stopped.
Gaheris was watching me. His eyes were afraid. I said "It was
Medraut who killed Lamorak?"

He swallowed. "It was an attack from behind. If he'd only
used a sword, I might have done something, had time to
make Lamorak move... But it happened so fast... Poor
Gavin didn't even see it." He stopped, passed a hand across
his eyes. "I'm gabbling. Sorry. Yes, it was Mouse. He shot
Lamorak in the back with a crossbow. Neither Gavin nor I
could do a damn thing about it." His voice cracked. "And I
can't make myself forgive him." His eyes were dry, but the
look in them was terrible. I put my arms around him, and
held on, finding nothing to say. He rested his cheek on my
hair. Medraut had led him into betrayal. And Gareth had
helped him blame himself... Finally, I said "Does Gareth
know?"

"I don't know," Gaheris said. "And it makes no
difference now, anyway."

# Six

Despite Essyllt's apparent lack of interest, Marcus went ahead with his planned tourney. The entire household was thrown into amused disarray. Dinadan and several others were dispatched to spread the word. Brangwen embarked on an energetic reorganisation of the accommodations, driving Essyllt to a succession of day-long rides and picnics. It was very easy to become mysteriously detached from the main party on such excursions, I soon discovered, and remembered with distant pain how Gareth had vanished from Guenever's Maying. "Sweetheart," said Gaheris, "ride back to Camelot, and see him fly to be with you."

"Would you come with me?"

"I have bloody hands."

It was to be a small tourney, with jousts for love, and no prize greater than applause, and a seat at dinner beside Marcus. The older squires and knights elect were also to be permitted to enter the lists, and as a result it was agreed that all should bear blank arms. Tristan still absented himself, but Palomides made the trip, and was rewarded with one of Essyllt's sleeves to wear as a token. Dinadan, after much cajoling, appeared with an apron tied about him. He'd begged it off the chief cook, to whose venison pasties he had vowed eternal devotion. Marcus elected him 'most shameless' on the spot. A few days before the tourney, Essyllt had mock-solemnly presented me with a scarf embroidered with my own green Kinkenadron lion. Gaheris bore it for me, pinned to his shoulder. A handful of the local lords came over, and the meadows were gay with pavilions. "Who do you like as the victor?" I asked Gaheris.

"I don't know some of the neighbours. But most likely Palomides. Or Andred, if he's lucky. "

"Not you?"

"Me?" He laughed. "Kay says I have all the combat style of a duck."

For all that, he fought well, the first day, and I sat that night at dinner with the victor's wreath of roses in my hair. The second day, the wreath adorned, amidst much laughter, the greying head of the chief cook, while Essyllt tried (quite successfully) to console Palomides, who'd cracked a rib when his horse trod on him. Gaheris himself had taken a nasty blow on his left forearm, and kept dropping things.

The third day was the last, and the largest: it was for this that any long-distance visitor would aim to arrive. We were all up bright and early. Essyllt was in a state of high excitement: she'd convinced herself that Tristan would turn up. She had a new gown of deep rose silk, and kept fidgeting as we tried to lace her into it. She caught my hand as we went down to the stand, and pulled me to her. "I'm so glad you came to me," she whispered. "Are you happier, lovey?"

"Yes," I said.

"I knew it." She kissed my cheek. "Your Gareth will perhaps I earn to be more attentive in future."

I hadn't the time to go to the combatants' enclosure to wish Gaheris luck again. (I'd already done so once today, a little before dawn, as we rose.) I caught his eye as he waited by the rails, and smiled. He smiled back and saluted me, as I took my place amongst Essyllt's ladies. The heralds blew the first call, and the third day's contest began. There were a number of new arrivals. The blank shields made it difficult to identify them, but Palomides beside the queen recognised several, and kept us informed. One of them was Safere. I held my tongue, though my heart sank within me.

Palomides also provided a commentary on style. After an hour, I began to see why Essyllt always claimed he bored her. Dinadan, I learned, was erratic, Andred too nervous, Gauter prone to over-correction... It would probably have been fascinating to another knight, but I had trouble keeping my face straight. Essyllt yawned behind her veil. "And what about our first-day champion?" she asked, perhaps with a touch of malice. Gaheris had wrong-footed Palomides twice in the single combat.

"Heris?" Palomides missed her tone. "Too defensive. And he spends too long analysing his opponent's style. Used to teaching, rather than exploiting weaknesses"

Midday came and went. We munched on pastries and fruit in the stand, while the combatants battled on in the heat. Essyllt was sulking: there was no sign of Tristan. It was airless; dust rose from the field, coating skin and clothes. Gaheris was having another good day, although his wrist seemed to be giving him some trouble. He'd had a series of straightforward victories over local knights, and a longish successful combat on foot against Andred. Now he watched from the enclosure while one of the grooms watered his horse. He'd removed his helm; he looked hot. A further handful of newcomers had arrived and were arming up: there were perhaps ten or twelve rounds to go before the melee. Gaheris had taken Dinadan down just before lunch. In the mid-afternoon heat, he must now face the open challenges to hold or lose his position. I was worried, a little, about Safere. With Orkney rivalries, there was always an element of danger. In the enclosure, Gaheris re-fastened his helm, and mounted. Here we went again…

Mid-afternoon. Gaheris held on to his place. Essyllt had decided that Tristan wasn't going to put in an appearance after all, and was taking her mind off it by flirting with her husband. Palomides was sulking, in turn. Gaheris' encounter with Safere had come and gone: Safere now watched from the paddock fence. From time to time, our eyes met, and he smiled, cold and composed. The pages brought round fruit and cider. Only an hour or two now, before the king declared a halt. The day began, blessedly, to cool down. A final small party of latecomers appeared, and began to haggle with the marshals. In the break this caused, Gaheris rode over to the stand, visor opened. He was flushed and sweating: he hooked his shield over his saddle, and shook out his wrist.

"Does it hurt?" I asked.

"Only when I think about it. Mostly it's numb." He smiled. "That's the worst of bone bruises."

"I'll take a look at it, later," Brangwen put in. "I've a salve."

He bowed to her. "Thank you." A pause. "Man, you've hot summers in Cornwall."

"And very soggy winters," said Brangwen, as I handed him up my cider cup. He took it in his bad hand, used the other to lift my fingers to his lips. The herald sounded the recall. Gaheris quickly drained the cup, and returned it to me, before riding back into the field. I blew a kiss after him.

"Your majesties," announced the senior marshal, "Three new challengers." Essyllt looked up, and peered at the newcomers with sudden enthusiasm, hoping for Tristan. One of them was very tall: otherwise I could discern nothing to distinguish any of them. Marcus signalled assent to their participation, and there was a brief discussion amongst the newcomers as to ordering. Gaheris waited at his end, rubbing his arm.

The newcomers reached a decision, with some jostling and noise. A knight in plain blond armour rode into the lists. Gaheris caught my eye, and smiled, then lowered his visor.

Dust rose up around them as the horses thundered down the field. One pass, with no hit. On the second, Gaheris broke a lance on the challenger's shield. A third pass, and the challenger struck a glancing blow on Gaheris's shoulder. Gaheris pushed the tip aside with his shield, and the challenger, forgetting to let go, lost his seat. Gaheris reined in, and looked at Marcus.

The challenger climbed to his feet, and drew his sword. Marcus nodded for continuance. A squire came into the compound to take Gaheris' horse: another had already caught that belonging to the challenger. There was a pause. Then the combatants closed. Some instinct made me look across at Safere. This time, he didn't smile. There was something wrong with this fight… The challenger moved fast and angry. Gaheris was tired. He used his shield poorly: that arm was giving him trouble. I turned to Marcus. "Cousin, stop this fight."

"What?" He looked at me, perplexed.

"I've a bad feeling… Heris is hurt."

Marcus reached across Essyllt, and patted my hand. "He'll be all right, love. And no one's broken the rules." I looked at Essyllt, who shrugged. Then I turned back to the field.

To this day, I do not know exactly what happened, or how. My angle of vision was wrong. Gaheris remembers being wrong-footed, and clipping the central railing. And the challenger… He can recall only instinct-level sequencing of attacks. But what I saw was simple, Gaheris over-reaching, and stumbling into the barrier, the challenger closing in to follow up, perhaps a little too fast, and both men going down in a tangle of metal and shields and splintering wood.

There was a long stillness. No one moved. Then the challenger slowly rose to his knees. There seemed to be a great deal of blood. Safere had jumped down from the fence and was arguing with one of the stewards. The marshals came hurrying down the line. In the enclosure, there was an outburst of shouting, then a slight figure came jogging into the field, head uncovered. He was dark, and on his surcoat was worked the device of the pentangle. Gawain. Something wrong… I came to realise that Brangwen had her hands on my shoulders, and that I was struggling with her. "Llinos, wait!"

"Let go." It was simple, if undignified, to slip under the rail. I heard Essyllt call after me as I gathered up my skirt and ran. None of the stewards tried to stop me.

Gaheris had still to move. Blood spread beneath him, and I couldn't tell its source. "An artery severed," said Safere's cool voice in my ear. "Your veil, Lady Llinos, and that small knife." I handed him the items, numbly, and dropped to my knees. The challenger was beside me, struggling with his helm. A moment, and a hand touched my shoulder. Gawain.

I said "Is he dead?"

Gawain looked at me oddly. Then he turned to the challenger. "Will you let me do that, man? You've your wrist-strap caught in the lacing of your aventail." His fingers moved deftly over the offending area.

I caught his arm. "Gavin, is Heris dead?"

He turned and stared. I said "There's so much blood… he hurt that arm yesterday in the melee." Gawain had gone white. "Gavin, what's wrong?"

"I should have known him." He sat back on his heels. "But Gari would have it was Ironside." He swallowed, and glared at the challenger. "Now will you see where your jealousies have brought us!"

Gareth finally dragged his helm off. He was as pale as his eldest brother. Weakly, he said "I didn' t know… I thought…"

"Oh, you're a mighty man for thinking," Gawain said. "And for assuming. And here's Heris paying for your assumptions again." I remembered Agravaine all those weeks ago, accusing Gawain of favouring Gaheris, and I put my face into my hands.

Without looking up, Safere said, "Will one of you cease quarrelling, and summon Dame Brangwen?" One of the stewards ran back to the main stand.

Gareth said "Is he…?"

"He lives," Safere said. "No more can I tell you: I regret I am better acquainted with necromancy than any healing art." I think we all stared at him. "Prince Gawain, you have steady hands. You might assist me by removing his helm." Gawain moved to do so. Gareth reached a hand out to me, hesitated, withdrew it.

"Llinos." He stopped, swallowed. "Sweetling, I swear I didn't know."

All those nights without him, and now I could not look at him for crying. He said "Gavin's right. I was jealous. I didn't think. I saw him kiss your hand, and he was wearing your token…"

"It was combat for love," I said, and he fell silent. Gawain and Safere had removed Gaheris's helm. He was unconscious, and a bad colour. I touched his hair with my fingers, and sobbed.

Perfume surrounded me, and a swirl of soft fabric. Essyllt's warm arms closed about my shoulders. "Come away, lovey," she said, gently. "There's nothing we can do here."

Later on, Safere came to the queen's solar to report. He'd washed his face and hands beforehand, but here and there on his clothing were bloodstains, and he looked tired. I was afraid to ask. Essyllt held my hands and said, "Well?"

"He lives." Safere hesitated. "The sword-cut severed the tendons as well as the artery, and the wristbones are crushed. The arm is broken, and also the shoulder. Prince Gawain says he's had a fracture there before." I remembered that: Christmas five years ago, when Lamorak had fallen on him in practice. Safere continued "Also several ribs. Those and the shoulder will heal. The arm as well, probably. The rest..." He hesitated, and looked at me. "He's going to lose that hand. With the tendons cut, he'd never use it again anyway."

We had found Lamorak's white pavilion, and won relief from cold and hunger. And Gaheris had looked down at me, and vowed that should there be a price, he would take it upon himself. I swallowed, and stared back at Safere, who had known that we were lost in the forest. I said "Did you know that this would happen?"

"No."

"But..." I stopped. "Why are you doing all this?"

He ran a hand through his hair. Then he said, "Lamorak. Is there another reason? I loved him, but he thought himself in love with your Gaheris."

I think Gareth tried to see me later that night, but Essyllt turned him away. She treated Gawain the same, but a little before midnight another visitor was permitted entry. Very tall, taller even than Gaheris…

Kay the seneschal kissed both our hands, while I said, "But why are you here?"

"Common sense," he said, accepting a chair. "We had a message from the queen of Cornwall that you and Heris had turned up here, and I wasn't about to let Gawain and Gareth go charging about by themselves. The Orkneys," and here he favoured Essyllt with a satirical glance, "have no sense of proportion."

I looked at Essyllt in turn. "*You* sent a message?"

"I wrote to the King of Logres," she said, defensively. "I thought someone might be worried. And," and she looked down, "I thought that husband of yours could use a lesson."

"Good intentions," said Kay, crossly, "are more likely than the Saxons to send the lot of us to early graves. Not," and here he turned his dark look on me, "that I'm overly impressed by all this rushing about in fits of panic, either. It wastes a lot of time, and it never seems to turn out well. Just look at Lancelot."

I looked at Essyllt, who gazed back at me blankly. Kay added "Not that Gareth was much better, moping around at court. He used to burn everything when he was a scullion, too." He caught sight of our faces, and sighed. "My wife says I'm about as sympathetic as a lump of granite. But someone had to come along and mediate between Gareth's idealism and Gawain's brotherly love. Just sorry not to have done a better job."

"Kay," I said, "tell me about Lamorak and Gaheris."

He looked at the floor. "Nothing to tell, really. It was no one's fault, what happened." He looked at me. "But I don't think anyone could have prevented it, either."

"I have no right to ask," said Gareth, "but I beg that you will hear me out just this once." He spoke to the floor, on his knees before me in my small room. I'd found him there when I returned from a fruitless visit to the infirmary. He had kissed my hem. He looked pale, and tired, and unhappy. It seemed likely Gawain had been on at him all night. I longed to comfort him. I was afraid to try. He said "I've wronged you so much. I don't know where to start."

"Sit down somewhere," I said. I sat on the bed, pleating the coverlet with my fingers. Gareth rose, and found a stool. We looked at each other in silence.

He said, softly, "I love you so much." I looked down. He went on, "I am so ashamed."

"For loving me?"

"For mistreating that love." He swallowed. "You were so unhappy, when the baby died, and I felt so useless. You didn't seem to need or want me any more. I didn't know what to do." I twisted my hands in the coverlet, and tried not to cry. Gareth said, "I wanted so much to help you."

I looked up. I said "I was afraid. It hurt so much... I needed to hide."

"Yes." He sighed. "But I didn't understand, then. I am so sorry."

He, too, was close to tears. I wanted to go to him, to hold him and take the pain away.

I stayed where I was. I said "I shut you out. I realise that."

"I love you," Gareth repeated. He rose, and went to the window, "Everything was such a mess, I don't know. Agrin at Heris's throat over mother's death, and then Lamorak..." He paused, drew in a long breath. "I don't know how to explain. I was angry with the whole family for Lamorak's death, but Heris... Perhaps I needed someone to blame for my own misery, and he was there. Lamorak loved him, you know."

"Safere told me."

"I don't understand Heris. I never have. I was six years old when he was sent off with Gavin as a hostage to Arthur. I remember he hated thunderstorms and winter greens. He was always the quiet one. He never seemed to want anything, or at least he never mentioned it if he did. He still doesn't, come to that." Gareth turned, and leant on the wall. "He's so meek. It's easy to blame him for things."

"For Lamorak," I said.

"For Lamorak." Gareth looked at the floor, shaking his head. "I couldn't understand how he could stand by and let Lamorak die... Gavin told me, over and over, that Agrin threatened to drag him bound if he didn't go willingly. I still don't understand it. I'd have fought Agrin to a standstill."

"Gaheris," I said, "has no faith in himself."

"Oh, God. And we all bully him, I know. You should have heard the fights Gavin had with Kay on that subject on the way down here." He looked up again. "Anyhow. The

Lamorak business. I could give you any number of rationalisations. Heris didn't do as I would have done. He knew who was responsible, yet he brought no complaint. They're all excuses. The truth is much simpler. I was confused, and lonely, and I wanted to hit out."

"What happened?"

Gareth swallowed again. "He was blaming himself, of course. If Heris had been around at the time of the Flood, he'd have found a way to feel responsible for that, too. So he offered his life to Aglovale de Galis right in front of everyone, and Aglovale refused him and made peace, of course… It all looked so empty, so false… I lit into him for it." He stopped, rubbed his hands together. "I've never fought like that with any of my brothers before. I called him every name under the sun, I threatened to disown him, I raked up every grievance, large and small, I could think of. Jesu, I even accused him of collusion in Pellinor's death. And he took it. He made no attempt to defend himself. When I finished, he just looked at me, and said 'Agrin won't kill me on account of common blood, and Loval de Galis is too damn forgiving. Perhaps you'd care to do the job, and put me where I can do no more harm'." Gareth stopped again, and passed a hand across his eyes. It was all I could do not to go to him, "I should have realised then that he was as miserable as I was. But I only saw what I wanted to."

I said "I'm so sorry. If I'd had the courage to come back to court…"

"What?" Gareth came to the bed, and sat down beside me, taking my hand in his. "Sweetling, this is no more your fault than it is Heris's. I was unhappy and I made a terrible mistake." He looked down. "The first in a whole series. A few days after that, I found Luned crying on the terrace. She told me it was over Heris, someone had taunted her... To this day, I don't know if that's true. But I felt sorry for her. I was lonely myself, and here was someone who needed me, someone I could help. My brothers were either avoiding me, or acting like I was crazy, and you didn't seem to want me around." I gave a small gasp, and he put his arms around me. "I'm sorry," he repeated. "I never meant for anything to happen with Luned. I suppose I thought I was being brotherly, to begin with. But over the next few weeks..." He stopped, pulled a face. "She needed me, it seemed. More fool me for being so selfish. I've hurt her, too. I didn't love her. I don't even like her, much. But I enjoyed the comfort."

I straightened in his arms. "I understand that."

"You do?" He looked surprised. I don't expect you to forgive me, but..."

"The business between you and Heris isn't for me to forgive, but as to the rest..." I inhaled. "Let me go, Gareth. There's something I have to tell you, too."

He released me, slowly. He looked vulnerable, a little afraid. I said "What did you think, yesterday, when you saw me at the tourney? You said you were jealous."

"Yes." He looked rueful. "I'd given you every reason to give up on me. And when I saw someone else with your token... Gavin's right. I just jumped to conclusions. That old fool Ironside lives locally, and he was so keen on the idea of you that he besieged you for two years…" He blushed, and looked at his hands. "What you must think of me."

"Well, I don't much care for your opinion of my taste." He glanced up, and smiled quickly. I went on, "But you weren't entirely wrong. You mistook the man, but not the situation."

There was a short silence. Gareth stopped smiling. He said, softly, "Paid in my own coin… No, I deserve it." He wrapped his arms around himself. "You and Heris?" I nodded. "Are you in love with him? I can bear anything but that. I think I can bear it."

"No."

"I wonder what Gavin would call this?" Gareth's tone was light, but his voice shook. "Ironic symmetry? I don't even have the right to ask you why."

"It wasn't revenge," I said, "whatever it looks like. Heris, at least, wouldn't do that." Gareth looked at me sidelong. I continued. "The first time was almost an accident. We'd been lost for days in Surluse forest. Everything was very strange; it just happened, somehow. And later… He made me feel safe. Reassured." I put a hand on Gareth's arm. "It wasn't his doing."

Gareth's expression was strange. Raggedly, he began to laugh. "Well, I can't say a word about it; it would be sheer hypocrisy… I'll lay you straight odds Heris tries to shoulder all the blame for this, too, once he's conscious. Let me see: he'll say something like he wronged me with my wife, and the loss of his hand is only fair punishment?" He stopped, abruptly, and drummed his fingers on his knee. His hand shook.

I said "You're angry."

"Bloody furious." He turned. "I know I don't have the right to be. It's all right. I'll be better in a moment."

We sat in silence for a few minutes, while he drew in several long breaths. Then he said "Are we all right, do you think? Or are we over?"

"I love you," I said. "I don't know about the rest."

He took my hand, and kissed the fingers.

A long time later, he kissed the corner of my mouth, and said "What about Heris?"

I stiffened in his arms, looked at him warily. He sighed, and continued, "I meant simply that he's in a hell of a mess, and a lot of it's my fault. What can I do?"

"I don't know." I stroked his face. "He thinks you're right to condemn him: if you apologise too much, he'll probably feel worse."

"He's lost a hand," Gareth said, and shivered. "I shall live with that forever."

I thought about Gaheris, kind and straightforward and alone. I said, "I think the trouble is inside him. You can't rescue people from themselves."

"I love my brother," Gareth said, and started to cry.

It was almost a fortnight before I was allowed to see Gaheris.
Brangwen had barred the whole family from the infirmary on
the (perfectly reasonable) grounds that we were not
conducive to peace and quiet. Gawain took it surprisingly
well; it was Gareth who fretted and fumed, and tried to bribe
Kay, fruitlessly, to take messages. Before being let in myself, I
practically had to swear on the Bible to be calm and sensible.

"Is he still in danger?" I asked.

"No more than usual, with a family like his," said Kay.

He looked awful, frankly: his colour was poor, and he'd
lost a lot of weight. His left arm and shoulder were heavily
bandaged; the arm ended in a neatly wrapped stump. The
sight of it made me want to weep. Seeing me looking, Gaheris
smiled and said "It's all right. I just have one arm a little
longer than the other."

"Oh, Heris." I sat on the bed and kissed him, carefully,
on the cheek.

He said, "I feel better than I look. I nearly had a relapse
yesterday, when Kay brought in a mirror." That made me
laugh. He took one of my hands in his single one, and said
"You are all right, aren't you?"

"Yes. Yes, I'm fine."

"I'm glad. You deserve to be happy." He hesitated. "Did
Gareth…?"

I said, hastily, "Gareth sends his love. He's probably going to drive you berserk, trying to wait on you once Brangwen lets him in here."

"There's something to look forward to."

There was a silence. I held onto his hand, and looked into the dark- circled grey eyes. "You know, Heris, just for the record, I love Gareth…"

"Aye."

"No, let me finish. I love Gareth, so I can't really blame Luned for loving him too. But all the same," I reached out, and touched his face with my other hand, "I think she's blind, not seeing what she has in you."

It was another two days before Brangwen let Gareth visit, and then only for five minutes, and under her supervision. I hovered outside.

Gareth emerged red-eyed and distressed. "He apologised, Llinos. *He* begged *my* forgiveness." He stopped, and swallowed. "I'm beginning to see why Gavin gets so angry with him. Of course, I stopped him, and tried to explain, but Brangwen threw me out."

"Good for Brangwen," I said.

# Seven

I don't know if, in the end, Gareth ever did get the chance to have the conversation he wanted with his brother. I rather think he didn't. It was painfully apparent that Gaheris was distressed by the whole business, and in the end I suspect they simply agreed to both stop apologising. Neither knew quite what to say to the other, and Safere, who might have been able to throw some light on Lamorak's motives in the matter, had simply disappeared again. Tension reigned for some time between Gareth and Gawain, but the latter could never stay really angry with a brother for very long, and they eventually patched things up.

It was well into October before Brangwen pronounced Gaheris healed, and even then he was pale and easily tired. Kay, by that time, had returned to Camelot, but Gareth and Gawain and I stayed on in Cornwall. Essyllt was happy enough for the company. Tristan remained obstinately absent, and I think Gawain made a consoling substitute. She had hopes of pairing Brangwen with Gaheris, I think, but nothing came of it. Given the way her last scheme had turned out, I couldn't help feeling relieved. In mid-August, Alison finally made her way to me. She and Evan had not, after all, been able to raise the alarm. Around that last corner on the road, there had been another landslide. Alison had been found two days later, wandering dazed and feverish, by a shepherd. Poor Evan had been killed outright. I lit a whole branch of candles for him in Essyllt's small chapel.

We made our way back to Camelot, finally, in time for Christmas, riding in easy stages along the safe, interminable, coastal route. Gawain and Gaheris bickered amicably about sheep-rearing and politics, sword-play and root-crops. Sometimes, Gareth joined in too, and the king's highway rang with the sound of the king's nephews insulting each other. And two days before Christmas Eve, we came back to the court.

I found my sister Luned in her own room. She was packing. She halted when I came in, and stood there with a gown in her arms. She said "What do you want me to say?"

"I don't know," I said. "What do you want to say?"

She turned away, and laid the gown carefully in a chest. I said, "Where are you going?"

"The convent at Shaftesbury." She looked across at me. "I can't watch you with Gareth any more. And what I have with Gaheris isn't a marriage. It doesn't matter whether he's kind or unkind. I can't live like this."

"Are you so sure?" I said. "Gaheris…"

She held up a hand. "You know, sometimes I think the king got us the wrong way around, when he made our marriages. Oh, not you and Gareth, but… Laurel and Heris would go well together, I think: they could be nice, and sensible, and kind. Whereas I… Agravaine might beat me, but at least I'd have something to react to."

I found I had nothing to say to that.

Down in the hall, the family had gathered, checking and rediscovering each other. From the gallery, I could hear Agravaine winding up to lecture Gareth about injuring brothers. Gawain the mediator stood in between, putting in occasional critical words to either side. Medraut was at his shoulder, looking as ever as if awaiting his turn. Gaheris, quiet as usual, sat on the foot of the stair, listening. I sat down beside him, and rested my elbows on my knees. He looked down at me, and smiled.

"Well," he said, "I've two days, I reckon, before Agrin starts in on me. Do you think I'll survive the anticipation?"

# About the Author

**Kari Sperring** is the author of two novels (*Living with* Ghosts [DAW 2009] and *The Grass King's Concubine* [DAW 2012], the novella *Serpent* Rose [NewCon Press 2019] and an assortment of short stories. As Kari Maund, she has written and published five books and many articles on Celtic and Viking history and co-authored a book on the history and real people behind her favourite novel, *The Three Musketeers* (with Phil Nanson). She's British and lives in Cambridge, England, with her partner Phil and three very determined cats, who guarantee that everything she writes will have been thoroughly sat upon. Her website: http://www.karisperring.com and you can find her on Facebook.

# Also by Kari Sperring

## Serpent Rose
### A Tale of the Rose Knight

"Sperring really gets into the dynamics of the Orkney royal family, to produce one of the most satisfying and sympathetic pictures of Gaheris I have ever seen... A really excellent short Arthurian novel."

*— Amazon reviewer*

There are four sons of Lot at court and Sir Gaheris knows himself to be the least of them. Yet the charismatic and headstrong young knight Sir Lamorak looks up to him, despite more obvious choices, and when Lamorak catches his mother's eye, Gaheris knows there's trouble brewing. Soon he finds himself at the centre of family tensions, deceit and tragedy. Can he prevent the bloodshed that seems inevitable?

Available as a paperback edition and as a numbered limited edition hardback signed by the author.

"Kari Sperring's prose is elegant, her storytelling impeccable, Gaheris is a sympathetic character. I would have been happy to spend more time with him." *— Amazon reviewer*

www.newconpress.co.uk